IRENE N. WATTS

TUNDRA BOOKS

Text copyright © 2013 by Irene N. Watts

Published in Canada by Tundra Books,
a division of Random House of Canada Limited,
One Toronto Street, Suite 300, Toronto, Ontario M5C 2V6

Published in the United States by Tundra Books of Northern New York,
P.O. Box 1030, Plattsburgh, New York 12901

Library of Congress Control Number: 2012947609

Library and Archives Canada Cataloguing in Publication

Watts, Irene N., 1931-
Touched by fire / Irene N. Watts.

ISBN 978-1-77049-524-1. – ISBN 978-1-77049-525-8 (EPUB)

1. Pogroms – Ukraine – Juvenile fiction. 2. Triangle Shirtwaist
Company – Fire, 1911 – Juvenile fiction. 3. Book burning – Germany –
History – 20th century – Juvenile fiction. I. Title.

PS8595.A873T69 2013   jC813'.54   C2012-905817-3

We acknowledge the financial support of the Government of Canada through
the Canada Book Fund and that of the Government of Ontario through the
Ontario Media Development Corporation's Ontario Book Initiative. We further
acknowledge the support of the Canada Council for the Arts and the Ontario
Arts Council for our publishing program.

ONTARIO ARTS COUNCIL
CONSEIL DES ARTS DE L'ONTARIO

Edited by Sue Tate
Designed by Rachel Cooper

www.tundrabooks.com

Printed and bound in the United States of America

1 2 3 4 5 6   18 17 16 15 14 13

For Chaim Pinchas Levine
and Gentry James Williams

"Let 'em burn. They're a lot of cattle, anyway."

Inspector H.F.J. Porter quotes a factory owner's response
regarding the use of fire drills, March 1911
– *The Triangle Fire* by Leon Stein

Kiev, Russia, 1905-6

I

POGROM

My nightmares began after we had to leave the shtetl, the village where my brother, Yuri, and I were born. That was four years ago, when I was five. I had heard the word "pogrom," but I did not know what it meant.

Now I know, because I was there when it happened. It is hard to forget the broken shutters and windows, torn from their frames. Our front door was blue. Papa had just finished painting it in my favorite color – blue, like the blue of a spring sky or the blue of a duck egg – when the soldiers smashed it.

Here, in Kiev, we live in a gloomy part of the city. The house, which we share with three other families, is shabby. Our front door is old, scratched, and ugly, with peeling brown paint. It is not at all pretty, like the door of our first house in the shtetl.

There, everyone knew everyone else, knew their neighbors' business; nothing remained a secret for very long. My best friend, Malka, and I played in the narrow streets and in the small market square. We were happy. My little brother, Yuri, stayed close beside Mama, nibbling a carrot or digging in the dust. Mama sold vegetables, and Bubbe, my grandmother, her own braided challah bread. People came from nearby towns to buy or trade for goods. Grandfather Zayde, a shoemaker, was well known for making even the shabbiest boots look like new. The mayor himself brought his boots for Zayde to mend.

My grandfather taught Papa how to repair shoes too. "You never know when another trade might come in useful," Zayde replied, when I asked him why.

Papa can turn his hand to most things, especially if it means using a needle. He is a fine tailor, a master craftsman. Before we moved to Kiev, he worked at home on his sewing machine, making coats and shirts and waistcoats. Now he works in a shop. He cuts and sews from early morning to night, for someone else. Often Yuri and I are asleep before he comes home. Papa says he is saving rubles for a surprise.

"When will you tell us about the surprise, Papa?" I ask him.

"Be patient a little longer," he says.

I love surprises, but it is hard waiting for them.

———

This afternoon, after school, I go straight to the backyard to help Mama hang up the washing.

"Mama, why do you think the tsar makes us stay in Kiev? Our teacher does not like children who have come from the shtetl." I hand Mama Yuri's shirt, and she pins the sleeves to the clothesline. She sighs, and together we fasten the white Sabbath tablecloth up to dry.

Mama says, "The tsar can send us wherever he pleases. Sometimes he forgets about us for a while – that is a good time. When he remembers, he sends the Jews pogroms. Then it is not so good."

Mama wipes her hands on her apron. "Come, help me peel apples," she says. "We will make onion and apple dumplings for supper."

It is almost dark. Yuri rushes in, breathless from playing outside with his friends. He is sent to wash his face and hands for supper. Bubbe dishes up the dumplings we made, with sour cream. Papa and Zayde are already seated at the table, hungry after a long day at work.

Yuri's real name is Yaakov, but he refuses to answer to anything but Yuri because it sounds more Russian. He is almost seven, two and a half years younger than me and the apple of Mama's eye.

Between mouthfuls of food, Papa and Zayde complain about the latest increase in taxes.

Papa says, "Now we have to pay more, even for our Sabbath candles. Every day, there is something else to make our lives more difficult."

Zayde shrugs his shoulders. "Our 'little father,' the tsar, is not fond of Jews, and we live or die at his pleasure," he says.

"Is the tsar my father too? I am glad to have two fathers," Yuri says. He gets up and marches around the table. Then he salutes. "I will fight for the tsar and be one of his loyal soldiers," he says. "My teacher has a son in the army, and he came to school to show us his uniform. He told us about the army. 'Who wants to be a soldier?' he asked us. All the boys put up their hands, but I was one of the first. The teacher was pleased with me," Yuri boasts.

Mama grabs his arm. "That is quite enough of that kind of talk, Yuri. Say good night, and go off to bed like a good boy. It's late." Yuri marches out, still pretending to be a soldier.

Zayde sips his tea through a cube of sugar and stirs the slice of lemon floating on the top of his glass. "He is just a child. How can he understand what it means to be a Jew, in Russia? One day, he will dream of other things," Zayde says.

Zayde and Bubbe are Mama's parents. Papa's mother died soon after he was born. His father was sent far away to work down the mines. We never heard from him, except once, when Yuri was born. He sent a card, which Papa keeps in a special box. The grandfather I have never met wrote *I think of you all and send a blessing for the new baby son.*

When I asked Mama about him, she said, "Many people disappear in Russia." I feel sad for Papa. Sometimes, I have nightmares about all the bad things that happen.

Tonight, after supper, I take my doll out from the back of the dresser drawer, where I hide her – not to play with, just to look at and to touch for a moment, to make sure she is still safe. Before I get into bed, I put her back.

It is late at night. I can't breathe, my chest hurts, I'm afraid to open my eyes. Until I am properly awake, I cannot be sure if I am having a bad dream or if this is really another pogrom. I bite on my fist to stifle a scream. Then, slowly, so as not to wake Yuri, who is curled up next to me, I move to the edge of the bed. My brother is too young to remember the bad times.

Will the tsar's soldiers, the Cossacks, find us? Through half-open lids, I peer towards the window. There is a shadow. *Is it a soldier? Will he break the window or set fire to the house?*

Even the strongest door cannot resist fire. Everything in our house is made of wood. Cossacks like burning things. Wood burns easily – first the shutters, then the frames. I've seen how fast the flames can move, gobbling up everything in their path. Soon the flames will reach the roof.

This is the hardest part. I force myself to get out of bed, look around our small room, then cross to the window. There is nothing there, except a memory of that terror come back to haunt me. The curtains hang in their neat folds, and the house is quiet. If Cossacks were near, Mama would hide us in the cellar. I get back into bed, safe for now.

Yuri pulls the covers over his head. "Go away, leave me alone," he grumbles. My brother is always fighting someone or something, even in his sleep.

I lie awake and remember how the air was full of smoke. I heard the neighing of the horses in terror in the barn. I remember the sound of their hooves, hammering, kicking against the stalls, as they tried to escape. Then the smell after the barn burned down, with the animals still inside. I remember it all: the soldiers' laughter as they shredded the bedding, which had been left to air outside the windows. I remember the feathers, drifting down like snowflakes, long after the Cossacks had gone.

Our little houses burned. It was a long way to the river, and the flames spread too fast for our men to quench them. They could not outrun the fires or the soldiers.

My friend Malka and I had been playing with our dolls by the stream, near a clump of trees at the edge of the village. We dropped everything, held hands, and ran. Malka wanted to go back for her doll; mine was in my pocket. I waited, calling out to her to hurry, but she fell down. I ran to her and told her to get up. Malka refused to move, so I stayed with her. We screamed until our fathers came and carried us away. Papa had blood on his face, where a whip had slashed his cheek. Mama cried and pushed us under the bed, next to Yuri.

This is what I dream, over and over again: a nightmare of fires and breaking glass. I hear the shrieks of animals and children. Malka and I are there, screaming like them. Since then, I don't play with my doll.

It is almost daylight. I get up and go into the kitchen, where Papa and Zayde are drinking their first glass of tea. I sit on Papa's knee, and my grandfather pops a sugar cube into my mouth. Papa lets me take a sip from his glass. Mama bustles in to start making breakfast.

"Not dressed yet, Miriam? Hurry up, wake your brother. You will both be late for school." She removes the bowl of sugar, putting it away on the top shelf of the cupboard.

"We are not living in the 'Golden Land' yet, Zayde," Mama says, but she smiles at him as if they share a secret.

The "Golden Land" Mama is talking about is America!

2

SECRETS

Malka lives near us. We walk to and from school every day, and we tell each other everything. One morning, she is not at our meeting place – the corner of our street – as usual. I wait a few minutes, and when there is no sign of her, I run and knock on the door of her house. Her mother goes out to work, but the woman who lives downstairs opens the door.

"What do you want?" she says.

"Please, is Malka here?"

"The family has moved away." She shuts the door, and I hear her fasten the chain.

All day, I wonder and worry about what could have happened. Twice the teacher raps my knuckles for not paying attention. Malka's desk is next to mine, and my eyes fill with tears, seeing it standing empty.

At the end of the day, I run all the way home. "Mama, Mama, Malka is gone! Do you know where she is?"

Mama hugs me. "I am sorry, Miriam. Malka and her family have left Kiev. Moved somewhere else. I don't know where they've gone. Sit down, and we'll drink a glass of tea together. Try not to be sad." She pours us both some from the samovar, then reaches for the sugar bowl on the shelf and lets me help myself. Mama strokes my hair.

Where can this somewhere else be? Why didn't Malka tell me she was going away, when her family came for supper last week? Didn't she know? When our fathers talked in low voices, I overheard the words "bribe" and "border," so perhaps they are in another country. *Have they gone to America?*

Everyone talks about going to America – the Golden Land, they call it. They say, there, that no one goes hungry, that they eat sugar and chicken every day. I listen to Mama chatting to the neighbors. Sometimes, one of them receives a letter from a relative who has crossed the ocean and shares the news.

"'*Imagine,*' she writes, '*I can walk anywhere – to the park, to market – and enter any shop I want, without fear. I speak Yiddish with my friends, even in the street. I go to the library to read a newspaper, free! I can hardly believe it – the American policeman who walks up and down our street smiles. He speaks to my little girl: "Isn't it a fine day for a stroll?" he says.*'"

Pogroms happen in cities too, not just in small towns and villages. I hope the Cossacks forget about our street, if they come to Kiev. Papa says that this has been a bad year for pogroms.

A few days later, Bubbe and I are alone in the kitchen. She is teaching me to bake bread. She and Mama have been keeping me busy, to stop me from feeling sad without Malka.

"I have something to tell you, Miriam," Bubbe whispers. "It is about Malka and her parents. I know how much you miss your friend. Will you promise to keep it a secret?"

"I promise, Bubbe. I won't tell anyone."

"Zayde heard the news from a man he is making a new pair of boots for. I asked him how the man could afford new boots, made of Zayde's finest leather. It seems the man was paid well for helping Malka and her parents to cross the border. He hid them under some potato sacks in his cart. Who knows? By now, they might be on a ship to join their son and daughter in America!"

I hardly remember Malka's older sister and brother. They left Russia a long time ago. All I can think of is, my best friend has gone away too. *Will I ever again find another friend like Malka?*

A few days later, Papa comes home from work earlier than usual. He looks happy.

"Tonight," he says, "I shall make an announcement." *Are we going to find out about Papa's surprise at last?*

After we have finished our supper of potatoes, salt herring, and freshly baked black bread, Mama brings in the samovar and pours tea. We sit waiting for Papa to speak. Bubbe has taken off her cooking apron, as though we are expecting company. Mama's cheeks are flushed; her eyes sparkle. My mama is very pretty, with brown shiny hair and dark blue eyes – sometimes they almost look black. My hair is brown and shiny too. Mama says I have Papa's eyes – eyes that can melt a stone. I don't think that's true. Yuri gets away with much more than I do!

We wait for the great moment. Papa does not like to be hurried, even when he has a big order of shirts to sew. He puts his hand inside his jacket, where I know he has stitched a secret pocket, and pulls out an envelope.

Is it full of rubles? Rubles enough so that Mama will not worry when the rent man comes? Rubles to buy cloth to make something new to wear for Pesach, the feast of Passover? I would so much like to have a new dress. I can hardly wait.

Yuri fidgets – he wants to go outside and play before it gets dark.

"Come, Yuri, sit beside me," Zayde says. He strokes his beard, which is streaked with gray. Papa's beard is still black, like his hair. Yuri looks just like him. Papa opens the envelope and takes out three tickets, waving them in the air.

"Do you know what these are for?" He looks at us.

Yuri jumps up and down. "Tickets to go to the circus, Papa?"

"Tickets, you are correct, but they are not for the circus."

Yuri sits down again, disappointed. He longs to see the horses, acrobats, and wild animals.

"Are they tickets for the train, Papa?" I ask him.

"Who is going on the train? Why are there only three tickets? We are six in our family," Yuri shouts. The others turn and look at my brother, smiling, as though he has said something wonderful. I try not to be jealous of him getting all the attention.

"Quite right, my son," Papa says. "The first three tickets are for you and Bubbe and Zayde. We are all going on the train, but you three are going first. Mama and Miriam and I will come very soon. We are going to live in Berlin, in Germany, which is the first step of our journey. Then, when we have saved enough money, we will continue on to the Golden Land, to America. One by one, two by two, like the animals in Noah's Ark."

"America, Papa? Why so far away?" Yuri asks.

"Tsar Nicholas is our 'little father,' but does a good father burn his children? No, and in America, they don't let you burn. We will drink a toast to our journey and to a new and better life," Papa says.

Mama takes four glasses from the cupboard. Zayde puts a bottle of vodka on the table and pours a little of the clear liquid into each glass.

"*L'Chayim*. To life," the grown-ups say, clinking glasses. They smile. Papa and Zayde shake hands, and Mama and Bubbe embrace each other.

"I don't want to go to America," Yuri says. "I want to stay in Kiev, with my friends. I am a Russian boy, and I have decided, when I grow up, to be a soldier like my teacher's son. I will ride a big black horse and carry a sword or a gun. I will stay here and protect the tsar from his enemies. I will not go to America." He stands with legs apart, arms crossed, daring any of us to defy him.

Papa bangs his fist on the table – I have never seen him so angry. Mama and Bubbe look at each other, and Mama's hands fly to her mouth.

"You have decided," Papa says. "You have *decided* to be a soldier in the tsar's army. You *will* not go?"

Yuri stamps his foot. "Yes, I have decided, Papa," he says. "I will defend Russia from the tsar's enemies."

Mama tries to make peace. "Samuel, don't be upset – he is a child. He does not know what he is saying!"

"Then it is time my little son grew up," Papa says. "I want you to tell him, Sara."

I know what Mama is going to say, because Bubbe told me the story a long time ago. Another secret we share.

"Come here, Yuri," Mama says. She looks at him, putting her hand under his chin so that he cannot squirm away. "Once, I had a brother, an older brother. His name was Yaakov, and you are named after him. When he was not quite twelve years old, he was taken from us by Tsar Alexander. His soldiers came and stole him away. It had been the law in Russia for many years to conscript Jewish boys and make them join the army for twenty-five years. They snatched little boys as young as ten, sometimes. . . ." Mama wipes her eyes and cannot go on.

"My son never came back to us, Yuri," Bubbe continues. "Even though that law is abolished now, if someday the tsar wishes . . ." She does not finish her sentence, but in a moment goes on speaking. "It can happen again – today, tomorrow, next week. The laws against us, like pogroms, never end. Every day they make another, and who has enough rubles to bribe the police to look the other way?"

"If Papa says it is time to leave," Mama says, "then we go. Tell him you are sorry, Yuri." Her voice is firm.

My little brother hangs his head. He whispers, "I am sorry, Papa."

Zayde says, "I will need a clever helper like you, Yuri, as an apprentice when we go to Germany. You have good hands, much too good to carry a sword or a gun. You will see, together, we will make the best shoes in the whole of Berlin."

Mama sends us to bed. I take Yuri's hand, and for once he does not pull away.

Berlin, Germany, 1906-7

3

SEEKING REFUGE

The train journey from Kiev to Berlin passes in a blur of sleep, musty air, rattles, and sudden stops and starts. We sit on hard wooden seats; the windows are sealed shut. Even when the train halts, we may not get out for a drink of fresh water. The garlic-smelling breath of the fat couple who share our compartment, the old man with his grandson – who never stops kicking the seats – and the crying, sickly baby, rocked to and fro by his tired mother, give me a headache. The excitement I felt as we began our journey has disappeared. I just want to get there. Mama insists I eat a little black bread and some cheese.

Papa pats my hand, smiling at me. He says, "Imagine the good meal that Bubbe will have ready for us." *But does she know when we are coming?*

I realize I need not have worried, as the train jolts to a halt. I see Zayde pacing back and forth on the platform, waiting for us, holding Yuri's hand. It has been lonely without them all, these last three months. I am so glad Papa will stay with us for a while longer. I know most families cannot afford to leave for America all at the same time. Usually, the father goes first. Sometimes it is the older children, like the two sisters who used to live next door to us. They went alone and send money back home to their parents and five brothers and sisters. I would never dare to travel across the ocean without Mama.

We climb down onto the platform, and the guard shuts the doors behind us. We are here in Berlin, at last. The train departs in a hiss of steam, still packed with passengers on their way to the port of Hamburg.

Zayde greets us with joy. "The train is only four hours late. Welcome, my children." Yuri jumps up and down with excitement and talks so fast that my head spins. Zayde has borrowed a horse and cart for us. He helps Papa load our belongings, and we are off to our new home in East Berlin.

"Many Jews have settled there," Zayde tells us. "Wealthy Jews live in their fine houses overlooking the parks and grand streets. But most of us who have escaped the hardships of Poland and Russia and Lithuania live in the Scheunenviertel, the Barn Quarter. Some Jews are just passing through, waiting for passage to England, Canada, or America. Others plan to stay forever."

Yuri says, "Yes, stay forever, that is what I want to do." Mama and Papa take no notice of his chatter. They are too busy listening to Zayde.

He says, "Everything you might want can be found on the main shopping street, this one, the Grenadierstrasse. The Barn Quarter is like a small town that people like us have made. We are tailors, butchers, bakers, and shoemakers. Some work out of their homes, others in shops. Some buy and sell from pushcarts. There are hotels and boarding-houses, restaurants offering dishes from many countries. People crowd together. It is a ghetto of our own making, and yet it is not. No walls shut us in or out. Many languages are spoken here – German and Yiddish and Polish and Russian. When the Gypsies come to the market to sell their wares, they speak a mixture of everything –"

"Mama, I like it here very much," Yuri interrupts, incapable of waiting another moment to speak. "The streets are named after soldiers. It is wonderful. Mikhail, my friend who lives upstairs in our house, and I go everywhere together. We march like soldiers along streets named for army corps – Grenadierstrasse and Artilleriestrasse and Dragonerstrasse. Maybe when I grow up, I will become a Grenadier."

I give Yuri a warning kick before Mama gets upset at this kind of talk from him. I tell him, "There are no Grenadiers

in America, Yuri, and that is where we are going soon."
He tries to pinch me, but Mama grabs his wrist. We turn
a corner.

Zayde says, "Here we are on Hirtenstrasse, and this is
number seven, our house." He stops the cart in front of a
narrow gray building, three stories high. Bubbe must have
been watching for us. There are cries of joy, questions,
hugs, and kisses. We follow Bubbe inside.

Bubbe says, "My cousin, Yetta, sends her regards. She
hopes you will be comfortable here. She lived in this apartment for many years. It is a stroke of luck that she decided
to move in with her daughter, in Frankfurt. The landlord
has raised the rent a little, but what do you expect? We will
manage. Now, come, I have made you chicken soup with
dumplings. You must be tired and hungry."

Mama and Papa sleep in one room; Bubbe, Zayde, and
Yuri in the second room. I'm on the couch in the living
room. There is a kitchen too, with a good big stove.

Tonight, before I go to sleep, I wonder why we don't stay
here, if Germany is such a fine place to live. *Why does Papa
still dream of America?*

As we settle in, Zayde tells us word has quickly spread in
the neighborhood that he is a good shoemaker. He mended
Yuri's friend Mikhail's boots and his father's. Mikhail's
father is a glass cutter and glazier. He carries his bag of

tools on his back from street to street in our quarter. We live on the ground floor of the house, and Zayde has put a sign in the window. It says OSTROVSKI – BOOTS AND SHOES REPAIRED AND MADE-TO-ORDER.

Zayde has set up his workshop in the storeroom below the kitchen. He says many small businesses are run out of people's homes. He and Yuri have whitewashed the walls, and Zayde put up a shelf and strengthened the legs of a table for his tools. Yuri spends many hours there, helping him. After school, Yuri shines the shoes Zayde has repaired and delivers them to his customers. He never has to go far – the Barn Quarter is not very big. Yuri says the customers often reward him with a slice of bread and jam or chicken fat.

Papa has rented a sewing machine. He works in the living room, where the window gives the best light. Papa makes shirts, coats, and waistcoats, and sells them where he can. Soon he hopes to be taken on at a tailor's. Everyone in the family helps to earn money for food, for rent, and for tickets to sail to the Golden Land.

Bubbe continues to give me cooking lessons. Everything will come in useful in America, they say.

The minute I get home from school, I start to work. I sew buttons on the blouses Mama embroiders. She sells them at a shop specializing in fine ladies' wear, lace, and linen. Frau Goldschmidt accepts only the very best work for display. Her business is in the center of the main shopping street.

People come from all over Berlin to buy the goods made in our quarter. Mama is teaching me to attach collars and cuffs to the blouses, now that I have mastered buttonholes. Sometimes I think if I have to finish stitching even one more buttonhole, I will scream!

Then Mama takes pity on me. "Go, Miriam, make some tea. We will rest for a little."

Whenever I am sent on an errand, I try to explore a bit. One afternoon, I went to the outskirts of our quarter and walked along the River Spree, which runs all the way through the city of Berlin. I went partway across the Palace Bridge – the Schlossbrücke – and looked at the statues of Greek gods and military heroes. Set in between them were smaller sculptures of strange, mythical creatures from under the water.

I got home later than usual, and Mama was worried, even after I explained to her that I'd been longing to see more than just our little bit of Berlin. She does not scold Yuri when he roams all over the place, and he's younger than me. It's not fair.

A girl in my class, who has a sister and a cousin in America, told me girls have much more freedom there. She said that more Jews live in New York than anywhere else.

Papa says we all have to learn English for our move to America. One evening, he brings home a teacher for us whose name is Kolya Seltzovsky. He is from Russia too. Since

Papa has started working for a tailor on Dragonerstrasse, he meets many people, and that is how he got to know Kolya. He came into the store to have the lining of his jacket mended. Papa has invited the young man to stay for supper. I set a place for him. Mama presses Kolya to eat, and he does not need much encouragement!

"We have plenty," Mama says, which is not strictly true. Luckily, Yuri is upstairs having supper with Mikhail and his family, so there is enough for our visitor. He eats a big bowl of potato soup with sour cream and two thick slices of bread. He is tall and thin, and his deep-set dark eyes seem to burn like coals. His smile makes him almost handsome. Kolya has good manners, and he thanks Bubbe and Mama politely for the good supper.

Papa asks him, "What has brought you to Berlin?"

Kolya says, "In Russia, I attended the Lithuanian University of Vilna. One evening, I went to hear some speakers at a political lecture. One speaker was from America, and his talk was about democracy. The place was crowded with students. As I was leaving, someone put a pamphlet into my hand. The police were waiting outside, and they stormed in. I dropped the pamphlet and stood on it. Many of us were arrested, just for attending the meeting. I was fortunate to spend only one night in jail. The guards beat me up a little, warning me that next time they found me in such company, I'd be kept in prison for a long time."

"So, now your name is on the police files," Papa says. "It is a miracle they released you, Kolya."

"Yes. When I got home and told my parents what had happened and they saw my bruised and bleeding face, my father insisted we pack and leave immediately. We took only a few essentials, told no one, and left our home. That night, we attempted to cross the border into Germany. I thought we were going to make it. I was carrying my little brother, Lev, on my back, when suddenly voices shouted to us to halt! My father told us to go on.

"He ran to draw the guards' attention away from us. Shots were fired. We got across the border, but my father did not. My brother has not spoken a word since – nothing, not a sound. The doctor says it is shock, and one day, when he is ready, he will speak again. Lev is only eight years old.

"Herr Rudolf Mosse, the publisher, has taken me on as an apprentice. How proud my father would have been to hear that I am working for the founder of a Jewish newspaper. In Vilna, I studied languages, so as well as Hebrew and Yiddish and German, I speak English. I hope to give English lessons in my spare time."

Zayde says, "You have chosen a fine trade. My son-in-law was lucky to find you." Kolya bows his head modestly and smiles.

So it is decided: Kolya will eat supper with us three times a week, and Papa will make him a new shirt and mend his coat. Zayde will repair his boots too. Kolya says his mother is taking in laundry – that way Lev does not have to be left alone.

Papa says, "If you bring me your brother's measurements, I will make him a new shirt also. Is it a bargain?"

"It is a bargain. Thank you, sir," Kolya says with a big smile. They shake hands.

Yuri has been standing at the door, staring at the stranger sitting in his place and listening to Kolya's story. I had heard his boots clattering down the stairs, but this stranger has kept him quiet for once!

Yuri says, "Your brother can come to play with Mikhail and me, if he wants. I am almost eight too. He does not need to speak; we will just practice marching."

Kolya shakes Yuri's hand. "Thank you for your kind thought. One day, when Lev is no longer afraid."

Yuri flushes. It is not often that our Yuri shows the kind heart that beats under all his bragging of becoming a soldier and going to war.

"Such a smile, he has," I overhear Bubbe tell Mama after Kolya leaves.

Mama says, "An apprentice does not earn much money. It is good that he comes here for a meal. How hard it must be for his mother to lose her husband and to make a living in a new country. And now she bears the burden of a child mute with fear. I hope he recovers soon."

Berlin, Germany, 1907-8

4

ENGLISH LESSONS

We look forward to our lessons after supper. Mama and Bubbe continue with their sewing. Kolya asks them to put their work aside. "You must concentrate," he says.

He teaches us important questions to ask and how to answer, so that when we go to America we can make ourselves understood.

"Where is this place?"

"How are you?"

And the answer is "I am well," or "I can't grumble."

"Where are you from?"

And the answer is "I am from Russia."

Mama makes us laugh. Today she asks, "Do you grow chickens?"

Yuri corrects her. "You keep chickens, Mama. Chickens are not the same as cabbages!"

I notice that Bubbe does not find it easy to join in. When she can't think of a word, she says it in Yiddish – the mix of Hebrew, German, Russian, and Polish she is used to. Bubbe smiles sweetly at Kolya when he corrects her.

The months pass. Almost a year has gone by since we arrived here. Our assignments for Kolya become more difficult. Today we must speak in English for one minute, about someone we admire. A minute seems like a long time. Bubbe talks to herself while she drops dumplings into the soup. I whisper my words as I walk to the butcher to ask for a lamb bone. Mama repeats English phrases over and over again, pounding and kneading dough, as she wrestles with the words. Anyone watching or listening to us would think we are a crazy family! Kolya encourages all of us.

I am the first to begin. I talk about my best friend, Malka, how much I still miss our talks and laughter. I say that I will never forget her. Then it is my brother's turn.

Yuri stands up to speak. "I admire Kaiser Wilhelm very much. He was born with a small . . ." he hesitates, seeking the right word, ". . . crippled arm, but when he was only eight years old, he had to learn to ride. He fell off the horse many times, because he had no balance. He tried again and again, until he succeeded. Now he is a fine horseman. He never gave up. I want to be like him and serve in his army." Kolya praises Yuri.

I look at Papa and can guess what he is thinking. Papa does not admire the kaiser. He says it is well known, in our community and abroad, that the kaiser despises the Jews.

Mama looks tired. I offer to make the tea. We are accustomed to having a glass of tea together before Kolya leaves.

One evening, Kolya is not his usual cheerful self. He does not tease us. He even refuses a second helping of cabbage rolls.

Bubbe asks him, "Is something wrong? I made them especially for you because they are your favorite. You look pale – are you sick? There is trouble at work, maybe?"

"The supper is good, like always, thank you," Kolya says. "I had some bad news today."

Papa says, "You are among friends. Share your sorrow, my boy. It will help you to speak of it."

Kolya falters, "Do you remember what happened in Kishinev?" The grown-ups look at each other, a look I dread.

Papa whispers, "How can one forget such a tragedy? It will always be remembered. We knew people who came from there. I cannot speak of it – so many dead and injured, so many homes engulfed by flames."

"I heard that five hundred Jews were injured in that pogrom," Zayde says.

Kolya continues, "Some good friends of mine managed to escape. They took shelter outside the city, in a small shtetl

– barely that – little more than a few houses, a barn, and a wooden synagogue. It was not far enough away. I heard today that the village was burned to the ground and again people died. A few were sent to a labor camp in Siberia. I ask myself, why? They had done nothing, except be what they are, who we are: Jews!"

"From one generation to the next," Zayde says with a sigh. "It is never-ending."

"Kaiser Wilhelm will never let that happen here," Yuri says. He looks shocked.

"You are wrong, Yuri." Kolya speaks to him as if to another adult. "Kaiser Wilhelm is well known to be a hater of Jews. He is a first cousin of Tsar Nicholas – both of them are like-minded on this. That is why your papa works day and night to bring you all to America. Why do you think it is the dream of all oppressed people to go to the Golden Land? In America, there is no kaiser, no tsar – only a president, who is chosen by the people. Jews are treated the same as everyone else. In America, Jews are free to be who they are and live without fear."

Yuri says, "I admire the kaiser. I don't live in fear. I don't believe you. . . ." If Yuri says one more time that he is going to be a soldier in the kaiser's army, I know there will be trouble.

Papa says, "Believe it. We live here like rats in a trap, so many of us crowded together. When it pleases a kaiser or a tsar to get rid of us, then it will happen. Not today or tomorrow, but one day the burning will reach here too. In America, my son, no one will burn us."

"It is late – enough of this kind of talk. I will make tea," Mama says, rubbing her back. She looks tired.

"Sit, Mama, it is my job to bring in the tea," I tell her.

The baby will be here in a few months. I can hardly wait. How I long for a sister – one brother is enough! But, as Bubbe says, "Boy, girl – as long as the baby is healthy and your mama stays well, that is all that matters."

Before I go to sleep, Papa's words stay with me. *Will the kaiser's troops come to chase us out of the Scheunenviertel?* All the houses have cellars. Perhaps they would not find us. I don't believe that it will happen. This time, I think Yuri is right. All the same, whenever I go somewhere new, I look for a place to hide or a door to run through, to get away from anyone who might harm us. I don't speak of it, but I think Mama knows.

Tonight, for the first time in months, the old dreaded nightmare returns. First I hear the sound of boots and horses' hooves on the cobblestones, then shouts and cries in a jumble of German and Russian. Windows smash, shutters splinter close by. In my nightmare, I stumble to the kitchen, where the curtains Mama made are charred. Sparks flare on the neatly folded smocks, ready for delivery.

They burst into flame, engulfing the room. We are trapped. I try to call for help, but the word sticks in my throat. *Can the others not smell the smoke?*

I force myself awake. No longer dreaming, I sit, stand, and walk into the kitchen. All is as it was before I went to bed. The samovar has cooled; the stove still glows, its embers slumbering. Barefooted, I lift Mama's shawl from the peg on the kitchen wall, hug it around me, and open the front door. Everything is quiet.

The air feels sharply cold on my bare legs. Nothing moves. How sad the Barn Quarter looks at night, with no one there. This is how it would be if no one lived here anymore. One solitary cart trundles into our narrow street. The old man does not notice me – he is bent low over his pushcart.

I wish my father would not talk to us about pogroms at bedtime. I would like to tell him so. No, better not.

Papa would say, "Since when does a daughter tell her father what he can talk about?" But in twenty-five years, when I am as old as Mama and have children of my own, I will tell my husband not to frighten them. I smile at the thought. *How will we look? Where will we be in 1933?* Pogroms will be a forgotten history lesson, and we will all be safe in America!

Berlin, Germany, 1908–10

5

DEVORA

There is frost on the windowpanes. Fresh snow covers the cobblestones. It is bitterly cold, but not quite as cold as in Russia. Only the big stove keeps our kitchen warm. Mama puts a shawl over her head to go out to the bakery.

Bubbe says, "Where do you think you are going, Sara? Do you want to slip? Here is someone all ready to run your errands." Bubbe shoos me out to pick up a crusty loaf from the bakery around the corner.

Tonight, Papa comes home late again. I bring him the bowl of soup that has been kept warm for him on the stove. He says, "We cannot keep up with the orders. The cold brings in new customers daily. They ask for a heavier lining, or better yet, a cape with fur trim or a new overcoat. I'll be working sixteen-hour days for the rest of the month. I have to return to the shop as soon as I finish this delicious soup."

"I never see you these days, Sam," Mama says.

"I miss you too, Sara. But I must work while the winter cold lasts. Hold out your apron." Papa pulls a small cloth pouch from the lining in his jacket. Coins tumble down into Mama's lap. "At the end of the month, there will be enough money to buy my ticket to America, with some left over for you, while I am away," Papa says, smiling at us.

"So much, Sam! How hard you have had to work," Mama says.

"It is for a good cause, Sara," Papa says. "It's for you and the children, for Bubbe and Zayde. A ship sails to America on March 7, and I mean to sail with her. In America, I will work even harder, so that you can all join me as soon as possible. Nothing is more important. Now I must get back to my waiting orders and my sewing machine."

Mama gives Papa a bottle of hot tea to take with him to the shop.

Yuri has slipped out, mumbling something about making a snowman with Mikhail. But I notice that he always finds an excuse not to be here when Papa speaks of the Golden Land.

January 25, 1908. Today is my birthday, and I am twelve years old. Zayde has made me a beautiful present, more beautiful than I could ever have hoped for: boots of the softest leather. Just to look at them makes me feel like a tsarina.

I throw my arms around his neck. "A thousand thanks, Zayde. I will keep them forever!"

"Try them on, Miriam," Zayde says. "Let me see how they fit. I made them a little big, to grow into, so that they will last you until you reach America. Wear them in good health, my child."

Bubbe baked a raisin and almond cake, which is my favorite. But the long-awaited gift, the best of all, arrives one week later, on February 2, 1908. Devora, my baby sister, has joined the family.

She is perfect. Her skin is smooth and unwrinkled, and black wisps of hair cover her head. Bubbe is sure they will turn into curls. We think her eyes are brown, but they are usually squeezed shut. Yuri is not very enthusiastic about another sister. He and Mikhail were planning to recruit the new arrival into their games, but even he admits that Devora is a good baby.

Papa finished her cradle just in time. You would never know that it is made from odd pieces of wood that he found in alleys, barns, and even outside our quarter. This winter is so cold that there is very little wood left lying around. People are desperate to find something to burn. I see them forage for kindling to put in their stoves. Papa and Zayde have hammered, planed, and varnished to make a perfect small cradle on sturdy rockers that fits Devora snugly.

Mama and I lined the cradle with soft muslin, and Bubbe
has embroidered three small nightgowns. Mikhail's mother
knitted a little blanket. It is so cold in the house that Devora
has to wear a cap and mittens day and night!

Papa leaves for the Golden Land soon. The ship on
which he will sail was built in Bremen and departs from
there. Papa will have a long train journey to the city before
going on to America. Mama's face grows sad as the time
draws near.

A few days before Papa is due to leave, he comes into the
kitchen, where Mama is stirring a stew for Shabbat. Devora
is awake for once, and he strokes her cheek. She stares at
him. Papa will miss her first smile, her first word, her first
tooth, and her first step!

Papa departs, laden with food for the long journey. His
bags are filled with everything Mama and Bubbe think he
cannot do without. How empty our small rooms feel without him. We avoid looking at Papa's chair. I move into
Mama's room with her and the baby.

Mama says, "We should look for a boarder. It will
help us to save for America and make up for Sam's lost
wages."

Zayde says, "I will ask around. A lodger is a good idea,
but it must be the right one. Not someone who comes and
goes at all hours, nor one who is full of complaints."

Two days later, when Kolya comes to teach us English conversation, Mama asks him if he knows of a reliable person who is looking for a place to stay. Preferably some-one from the Old Country, needing room and board.

Kolya says, "I am glad you mentioned this. By a strange coincidence, I just happen to know of a perfect person – one who is exactly as you describe." I see him wink at Yuri. "Can you guess who it is?" he asks.

Without thinking, I blurt out, "You?" Everyone turns to stare at me, and my cheeks grow warm.

"Seriously, Mrs. Markowitz," Kolya says, "I really *am* in need of a place to stay. Mother has just been offered a posi-tion as housekeeper to a doctor's family in Dahlem. It is in a fine part of the city, some distance away. The doctor's wife has no objection to my brother, Lev, coming too. He is ten years old now and can make himself useful by working in the garden, cutting firewood, and doing other chores. He has started to speak again. It makes no sense for me to keep our two rooms. I don't need much, and my appren-ticeship will not be over for a long while. Would you con-sider me, please?"

Bubbe claps her hands. She has always had a soft spot for Kolya.

Mama hesitates, but only for a moment. "You can sleep on the couch in the living room, Kolya. We can put a chair or two at the end, if your legs are too long."

This is the first time we have laughed since Papa went away. Gradually, we've become used to being without him. There are many families like us in the quarter, but I know Papa won't rest until we are under the same roof again.

6

LETTER FROM AMERICA

It seems as if we have waited months to hear from Papa, instead of only weeks.

"Maybe the ship was delayed. It happens," Zayde says.

Mama worries. "I am afraid to think of him all alone, without family, in such a big city – a stranger in New York," she says. "Perhaps someone has stolen his money. One hears such stories, thieves waiting to swindle newcomers." Mama looks as if she might cry.

Bubbe comforts her. "Sara, this is not like you. Your Sam is a man who has lived through pogroms, who has never allowed his family to starve, even in the worst of times. He is a smart man who understands people. Such a wonderful tailor, and he even speaks some English, thanks to Kolya! He will be fine. He has been there only a few days – he must find a place to sleep, to eat, to work. Then he will write; you will see. And it takes time for a letter to cross the ocean, then to reach us. No more of such talk. You are tired, Sara, go rest a little. Miriam and I will put everything away." Bubbe pats her shoulder.

At last a letter arrives. Mama calls Yuri to fetch Zayde from his workshop. Bubbe dries her hands and takes off her apron in readiness for the great occasion, and Devora gurgles in her cradle. We sit and watch Mama slit open the envelope. Mama sniffs the paper.

"Does it smell of Papa, of America, Mama?" Yuri asks.

Mama smiles at him. "A little of both," she says. Mama reads the letter aloud.

192 Ludlow Street
Lower East Side
New York
America
March 28, 1908

"My Dear Ones,

"I am arrived. I have a roof over my head and a place to sleep. The journey was long, and we did not reach our destination until March 25. I am told that newer ships can make the voyage in much less time. I will make sure that, when I am able to send for you, you will travel by one of these ships. They're from the Hamburg America

Line, which leaves from Hamburg instead of Bremen.

"You will want to know about the voyage, about steer-age. I will tell you the truth. It is not for the fainthearted. For over two weeks, we lived in a dark noisy place right above the engines. We men slept in wooden bunks, in tiers, many hundreds of us crammed close together.

"On each bunk was a straw and seaweed mattress and pillow (clean and new at the start of the voyage). The bunk was about 6 feet, 2 inches long and 2 feet, 6 inches high. It was for sleeping and for stowing our clothes, belongings, and the food we brought. You were right, Sara – no towels were provided. Even the drinking water was rationed. Some men crept up to the second class and got more water for us. Our thirst was unquenchable. Every day as I ate, I sent you my thanks for the fine bread, the apples, and the pickled herring you packed for me. The food they brought down to us was often cold by the time it got to the last men waiting in line.

"Yuri, you would marvel at the utensils they gave us. For each man – a knife, fork, spoon, and a tin cup."

"Why would I marvel at that?" Yuri interrupts and is shushed.

"Imagine a tin lunch pail, such as a worker might carry to his factory, but this one so intricately made, I had

never seen anything like it. The bottom part was for soup and to wash in. Salt water is good to get things clean, and seawater is all we had, though there was fresh water to drink. As the voyage went on, less of it was given out each day. On top of the bottom part of the pail, a small dish fitted in for meat and potatoes and, on top of that, one for fruit and vegetables.

"I was fortunate, for I had a top tier to sleep on. The men in the middle tiers were the worst off, and, yes, small quarrels and jealousies broke out, but there was companionship too. I made a friend – a man from Minsk, Boris Laski. His story was a sad one, for it was his second attempt to reach America. The first time, he was cheated, and his ticket was good for only part of the way. They put him off the ship in England. He had to work for eighteen months to earn the rest of his passage. When the weather allowed, he and I would climb the narrow iron ladder to the deck to breathe some air that did not smell of smoke and garlic and pickles. Also such smells that I do not want to write about. The weather was often very rough, and we went through several storms. Twice the steerage steward could not serve us our coffee, or bring down the huge kettle of soup or stew, until the weather cleared. But, my dear, dear family, it was all worth it to sail into New York Harbor, to see the great Statue of Liberty, with her crown of spikes like the rays of the sun, one arm lifted high, holding a torch of welcome to rich and poor alike, Jews and Gentiles.

"At last the day arrived when we had only to pass though Ellis Island to be in America. That is where we embarked. We were herded inside one of the big buildings, then into a large glass-roofed hall, where we were told to leave our luggage. Officials shouted at us in many languages to hurry and form lines, each line separated by railings. Like cattle, we were herded through many doors and passed from doctor to doctor, who prodded and poked, made us cough, breathe, or not breathe. They kept the worst for last: where we stood in long lines, waiting our turn before the final door, we heard the children whimper. You understand, my Sara, I do not complain – America does not need the sick or helpless. But to have your eyelids turned inside out, with hands not so gentle, well, it is far from pleasant. Those who had the dreaded eye disease trachoma were sent back or to a hospital ward to be cured.

"Chalk marks in different colors marked our clothes, a different letter for each problem, another for those ready to be questioned by an official. And such questions! How was one to know what answer to give? You will say a truthful one, and so I did, though many did not, thinking they needed a better reply. Or that it was a trick question, and maybe so, for if you said you had

*employment, would they refuse you entry for taking work
away from a citizen?*

"'Why have you come to America?'

"'How much money do you have with you?'

"'What is your trade?'

"'Do you have a place to stay?'

"'Have you relatives or friends in America?'"

Mama says, "We must study these questions and how to
answer them. Kolya will help us. How good it is that Papa
prepares us for what is to happen."

Yuri fidgets. "Come on, Mama, please keep reading."

*"With God's help, we were passed through, allowed to
pick up our luggage and climb onto the ferry. Boris had
an address, given to him in England by a landsman who
had an uncle in America. That is how we came to Ludlow
Street. We share a room in a six-storey house called a tenement building. We board here, getting a morning and an
evening meal. For lunch, a nickel buys milk and a slice of
cake or maybe a sandwich and a sour pickle. Many families live here and almost all take boarders. Some sleep in
shifts on two chairs in the kitchen.*

*"The very first morning in America, our landlady told
us about a job market, quite close to us, where people who
need a worker or those looking for work can find what*

they need. Boris was a peddler in Minsk, and this is how he will start again – peddle anything he can get. Cooking utensils, old clothes, whatever he finds. Already he has discovered where the garment factories and shops are, many of them near us. He says he can pick up cloth remnants and ribbon and sell those. All he needs to do is to hire a pushcart. Even better, he thinks if he goes door-to-door and asks to buy secondhand goods, he can sell them again in the market. This is a man with many ideas.

"On my first day, I counted my money, and after I had paid a month's lodging, there was enough left to rent a sewing machine. Boris and I looked at each other – we both had the same idea. I will sew shirts, caps, aprons, work pants, and Boris will sell them as fast as I can make them. We agreed to split the profits and shook hands on the deal. But everything takes time, and so I stood in the market on Hester Street and waited to see what I could pick up. A laborer on the wharfs, I am not, but when a man said he was looking for a presser in a factory, part-time to start, I said I could do it. A presser, so what is so hard? To stand and press the clothes and iron the suits and coats, it pays nine dollars a week. I look at the way the pants are finished – I would not sell them to my enemy, if I had one. If the boss asks me, I will show him what I can do. But I do not want to take a person's job away. Some immigrants straight off the boat – greenhorns,

they are called – say they are garment workers. They do not know one end of a needle from the other. Nothing is what they know! It is a disgrace! I will not be a greenhorn for long. And what do you think, Sara? We have a new name. At Ellis Island, the inspector could not understand when I told him Markowitz and wrote down Markov. It sounds fine to me, an American name. I hope you do not mind.

"They say that this year, 1908, is a bad year on the Lower East Side, a depression. What depression? I have work; every place you look, there are butchers, bakers, fish straight from the sea – fresh, salted, smoked. Stalls are loaded with any fruit you can imagine. Children are fed. The streets maybe are not paved with gold, but what an abundance of everything there is, beyond our dreams. I like it. I am glad to be here and to work for your arrival. I pray it will not be long. And what life is in the streets! Lights blaze night and day, and an elevated train takes you wherever you need to go. No one looks at you as if you have no right to be here.

"Never in my life have I written so much. Now it is almost time for Shabbat. We are all Jews in this house, some not so observant, I think. But this is how it is in America, first comes the need to make a living. I, too, will do what must be done, which is to become someone better than I was before. We are all equal in the sight of

the law – that is the blessing of America. It is the dream we have worked for.

"Do not expect long letters from me in the future. I must work to bring you all here. From time to time, I will let you know how things are. Write and tell me any little thing, everything, about the whole family. Learn as much English as you can. It will help, though Yiddish is spoken by almost every person I meet.

"Even without all of you here, I look forward to the lighting of the candles on Friday night, to the prayers spoken, a braided loaf on the table, memories shared over the years. You are in my thoughts.

"Your loving husband, father, and son-in-law,

"Samuel Markov"

Mama says, "I have never received a letter from your papa before. So we have a new name, well, it is not the first time I have had to change mine!" She folds the letter carefully and puts it in the wooden box where she keeps family papers and treasures. After today, there will never be a Shabbat when I will not see Papa's eyes in the candlelight and hear the words he wrote to us.

Zayde says quietly, "It is, I think, a country for the young, for those who want to start again." He and Bubbe go to their room. Mama tucks Devora into her cradle, though she has almost outgrown it. Yuri and I are left alone in the kitchen.

I ask him, "Don't you want to go to America too, now that Papa has told us so much about it? I can hardly wait." I wish my little brother, just once, would agree.

He scowls at me. "I want to stay here, with Zayde and Bubbe, with my friends. This is a good place. Yesterday, Mikhail and I went to the stables with his father, and we watched him repair a broken window. Mikhail and I helped him, then we were allowed to sweep the floor. I like the smell of horses. A man was grooming a horse – a big black one, whose owner is in the cavalry. One day I could be a captain in the kaiser's cavalry. I don't want to move again, to have to make new friends. I liked Russia, I like Berlin. No one asks me what I want to do. Papa says he likes it in America, but I like it here. He doesn't need me in his Golden Land, and it's not fair to make me move countries again. Soon I'll be ten years old. I know I will never change my mind. I'm going to stay!" Yuri rushes out of the room.

Yuri can't mean Papa doesn't need him. He needs us all, not just to help make a good life but because he loves us.

But Yuri is a boy, who must obey his parents. When Papa sends the tickets, Yuri will not have a choice.

Berlin, Germany, 1910

7

ANOTHER PARTING

It is almost two years since Papa left for America. He has missed so much. Devora is not the baby he remembers – she will soon be two. She is walking well and talks and talks, though we do not always understand her. We show her Papa's picture, and she says his name, but when she sees Kolya, she shouts, "Papa," and holds out her arms to him. Mama tries to explain that this is not her papa, but she is too little to understand. We all spoil her – she is such a good-natured little girl. If only she would not get sick so often. Bubbe says she will outgrow being delicate, but when Devora, Yuri, and Mikhail caught measles a few months ago, the boys were better in three weeks. Our poor little Devora has never really recovered her strength. Mama had to send for the doctor, twice. It must be a dangerous illness for Mama to do that. The doctor's visits are expensive!

He said, "The child needs fresh air, fresh milk, cream, oranges, grapes, and nourishing soups to build up her strength. I will call again in a week or two, Frau Markowitz."

Mama sits in the kitchen, her head in her hands. "Fresh air, what does he want – I should send the child out in the snow? She eats what we eat, good soups and stews. Who can afford to buy fruit in winter? This is not America." Mama is worn out from staying up half the night sewing. Frau Goldschmidt pays her so little. If only Papa were here.

My brother comes in, his cheeks glowing from the cold. He takes two oranges from his coat pockets and places them on the table in front of Mama. Beaming with pride, Yuri says, "These oranges are for Devora."

Mama looks at him strangely, almost as if she has not seen him before. She touches the skin of the oranges, picks one up, inhales the scent, and quickly puts it down again.

"Where did the oranges come from, Yuri?" Mama says.

Does she suspect something? Mikhail and Yuri are quick on their feet. A stall owner might not notice the absence of two oranges. The boys would not think of it as stealing, but as what the doctor said Devora needs.

"I earned the money for them, Mama," Yuri says. "Mikhail and I go to the stables sometimes to help out. I refilled the water troughs, swept up, and Mikhail cleaned the windows. I paid for the oranges out of my share of the money. How do you think I got them – that I stole them?"

"Come here, Yuri," Mama says and kisses him on both cheeks. "Your papa would be proud of you. Just wait till we get to America, Miriam. Your brother is going to be a big businessman. Thank you, Yuri. What a fine gift you have brought for your sister."

Gradually, Devora improves. She eats a little more, but at night I listen to her wheezing in her sleep, and no amount of goose fat rubbed on her chest makes any difference. Bubbe says she will get better when the weather improves and outgrow her colds and coughs. I hope it is true.

One afternoon in late January, just before Devora's second birthday and two days before my fourteenth, a letter arrives from America. The envelope is fat; it must be a long letter. Papa does not write often, but even when he does, he has not much news. He works, he saves, he misses us – it's all he ever says. Last time Papa wrote, he said he was glad that Zayde had taught him to mend shoes because, even during the strike of the garment workers, when he stayed away from the factory, he was kept busy repairing boots and shoes.

Mama opens the envelope and gives a little scream. "The tickets – he has sent three tickets! Quick, Miriam, run and ask Zayde to come here." There is a clatter at the stove, where Bubbe has dropped the soup ladle. I pick it up and wipe it. My grandmother sits at the table, her eyes glued to the envelope. Devora climbs up on her knee. Yuri and Zayde hurry in. I hold my breath in anticipation. Mama waves the tickets in the air, more excited than I have ever seen her.

"Listen," she says, "Papa writes he has rented an apartment for us in a tenement building, five floors tall but not a skyscraper. That is good, is it not, Zayde? It is on Clinton Street. He writes there is a little park quite near, where Devora can play. Imagine, such a good father that he should think of that. There are four rooms – two bedrooms, a kitchen/living room, and a front room – space enough for us all. Yuri, you will sleep in the kitchen, the baby with us, and Miriam in her own little bedroom. He writes there are four apartments on each floor and two toilets and a water faucet in each hallway. And there is gas lighting. Well, candlelight I did not expect in America!" She laughs a little. "With all of us there and working, Papa writes it will be no time at all before we can send for Zayde and Bubbe. Maybe we take in a boarder. After all, with four rooms, there is space enough. How much room does one family need to start with? Papa writes that the rooms are very small – small, big, what does it matter, as long as we are all together again?"

"When do you leave, Sara?" Bubbe asks.

Mama holds the tickets up to the light. "We sail from Hamburg on February 17 and arrive on March 1. The ship is called SS *Amerika*. Don't you think that is a good omen?"

My grandmother tightens her arms around the baby. She warns, "It will be stormy and cold at this time of year at sea. You must bring warm clothes, a good shawl. We do not have much time to get you all ready."

In the excitement, I had forgotten that the tickets are only for Mama and Yuri and me. Devora does not need her own ticket yet, but Bubbe and Zayde have to wait a little while longer before there is enough money for them to join us.

Mama reassures her. "The sea air will be good for Devora. The doctor advised fresh air – isn't that so, *Mamele*? The Hamburg America Line is one of the best. Papa writes the SS *Amerika* was built in 1905, so it is only five years old – almost new. It will not be as bad in steerage as it was in the older ships."

Yuri's face shows nothing of what he is thinking. He asks, "Can I go and tell Mikhail, please, and give him the stamps from the envelope for his collection?"

Mama hesitates, wanting us all around her on this momentous occasion. "Here, take them," she finally says, "but if you go outdoors, wear your coat and scarf and come home in an hour. Zayde has errands for you."

Yuri runs off with a quick thanks. He is only happy out of the house, it seems.

Mama sighs, shaking her head despairingly. "What do we do with him, Father? He has become like a stranger," she says.

Bubbe says nothing. She takes Devora out for her nap.

Zayde pats Mama's shoulder. "Let the boy go," he says. "Yuri needs to spend time with Mikhail, to get accustomed to the idea of separation. He will come to accept the situation. I am happy for you, Sara, and for the children, but we will miss you." He goes back to his boots.

I take the opportunity to speak to Mama. "Mama, may I ask you something? When we are in America, maybe I can work in a shop, in a factory, or a department store. Did you know that Macy's is one of the biggest stores in the world? I have heard all about it from girls in school. In America, there will be opportunities to learn new things and to meet other girls my age. What do you think, Mama?"

"We will have to wait and see, Miriam. What do I think? You are only fourteen years old, with your whole life ahead of you, and now, a sea voyage across the Atlantic Ocean. We will take things one step at a time. First we must settle in our new country, become good citizens, and help Papa all we can. We need to make a proper home and earn enough to send for Bubbe and Zayde. You will be my right hand, and if that means cooking and cleaning and helping me with a bit of sewing the way you do now, that is what we will do." Mama throws up her hands as if I have asked for the moon.

"Yes, I understand. Mama, please listen. I want to tell you something else. . . ."

"So speak, I am listening," she says, but she is rereading Papa's letter and only half paying attention.

"Mama, Yuri does not want to go to America. He has said so over and over again."

"Miriam, Miriam, you worry too much. You think I don't know how Yuri feels? I know, but when he makes new friends in America, he will come around. Yuri will be another pair of hands helping to earn money for the family. He will be proud to help his papa. He can do so many things – a bright boy like him. He will like to be useful, and we might be able to send him to an American school. He is not twelve yet. A boy needs to learn everything he can."

"Mama, Yuri wants to stay in Berlin awhile longer, to go on helping Zayde. Shoe making is a good trade, isn't it?" I say.

Mama looks horrified. "So what are you trying to tell me? That Yuri not come with us, when I have his ticket here? What do you think we have been working for? Are you crazy? Yuri comes with us!" Mama folds her letter, stowing it safely away with the tickets in her box. Our conversation is at an end.

She hands me the pile of neatly pressed and folded garments. "Miriam, take these blouses I finished embroidering last night to Frau Goldschmidt," she says. "Ask her to pay us up to date, please. You may tell her we sail for America in a few weeks." I hate asking for money, even more than finishing buttonholes, but at least I can go out for a while.

Mama says, "There, you think I keep you home too much. Look how responsible I think you are to trust you with an important errand."

A week later, Devora starts to cough and wheeze. Bubbe rubs her chest with goose grease, puts a cloth over her head, and makes her breathe in the steam from a basin of scalding water. Not one of Bubbe's favorite remedies seems to help. My little sister refuses to eat. I soften white bread in warm milk, add a few raisins, and tempt her with thin slices of apple sprinkled with sugar, but she turns her head away after a few bites.

Mama sends for the doctor again. Each time the money she has put away for our journey becomes a little less. The doctor looks at the baby, takes her temperature, listens to her chest. Mama tells him we sail in two weeks. Doctor Braun straightens up. I bring him a basin of warm water and a clean towel. When he finishes washing and drying his hands, he turns to Mama.

"Frau Markowitz," he says, "it is out of the question that this child can stand up to such a journey so soon. She needs building up – good food, rest, and quiet. There will be no fresh milk on board. Atlantic weather is rough, and overcrowded conditions can breed all kinds of illnesses.

She may succumb to any of them in her present state. You face a journey of many days. I advise you, most strongly, to postpone your travel, and, if this is not possible, to leave the little girl with loving relatives. After all, the child has her grandparents to care for her." He smiles at Bubbe.

"But the tickets have been purchased." Mama is agitated. "My husband has been working for two years to send for us." She speaks fast in her anxiety, her voice shaky. Then she is silent, waiting for the doctor to reassure us.

He considers, speaks, but it is not what we want to hear. "As your doctor, I can only advise you. You must do as you wish. Dear lady, supposing your little girl survives by some miracle, she still has to pass a strict medical inspection at Ellis Island. Children there have been hospitalized or sent back. Devora is a delicate little girl, but she will outgrow this condition if you allow her to. You will see, in a year or two, she will be much stronger. Here is a prescription for a tonic to increase her appetite. Good day." I hand him his hat and open the door for him.

What are we going to do?

That night Mama, Zayde, and Bubbe talk for a long time. The next day, Mama says they have decided to accept the doctor's advice. Devora will stay with my grandparents until we send for them. By then, my sister will be a year older and stronger, more able to endure the voyage. Yuri and I try to take it in. Mama is brave to heed the doctor. I can hardly bear to think of leaving my baby sister behind.

Yuri says, "I am really sorry, Mama, but I have an idea. If I stay behind and go on helping Zayde as I always have, I will find time to play with Devora. I'll make her laugh. When Papa sends the tickets, we can all come at the same time.

"I am doing well in school, Mama, and Bubbe and Zayde and I will practice our English. I can help out more at the stables and earn money. I don't need to go to America right now. I can wait." He smiles innocently.

Mama says, "No, Yuri, Papa and I want you to come now. Enough. No more of your ideas."

"Why won't you ever listen to me, Mama?" Yuri shouts. "I want to stay here, I like it, I am happy. I am sick of hearing about the Golden Land. Please, let me stay in Berlin."

Mama shakes her head. "Be still, Yuri, you have said quite enough."

He looks at Zayde.

"A boy must obey his parents, Yuri," Zayde says.

Yuri rushes out.

"He will come around, you'll see," Bubbe says. "Yuri does not like change. He doesn't mean it, Sara."

8

YURI

Mama and I have almost finished packing. We do not own very many valuables, but we divide them between us. I have wrapped one of our Sabbath candlesticks in a skirt inside an extra blanket, and Mama has the other one, concealed in the same way in one of her bundles.

Bubbe says, "Who knows what kind of people you will be traveling with on the ship? Better to be cautious."

Mama kisses her cheek. "You are right, as always, *Mamele*. I don't know how we will manage without you, even for a short time."

It is well into the afternoon before Mama and I have sewn our money inside our waistbands and skirt hems. There is not a great deal left because of the doctor's many visits, but Mama says it will be enough until we find work.

"We need to leave for Hamburg, so that we arrive in

plenty of time to board the ship. There may be delays, and who knows for how long? Suppose we have to find lodgings overnight? I can imagine lengthy waits, with hundreds and hundreds of people leaving at the same time."

Mama thinks of everything. She says I worry, but from whom did I learn about worrying? I hear an anxious note in her voice as she asks where Yuri is. She brings in the samovar and pours our tea.

"It's getting dark. Where can that boy have got to? I told him to be home long before this. I don't want a last-minute rush in the morning. We leave from Lehrter Station at 8:00 a.m., so we must be there well before the train leaves. Zayde says it is not a long journey to Hamburg – a little over four hours – and then the waiting begins to board the ship. We need to be prepared and ready early. This is no way to start out."

I think how selfish Yuri is being, worrying Mama in this way. It is hard enough for her having to leave Devora behind. Bubbe comes in, and Mama asks her if she has seen Yuri. Zayde warms his hands round the glass of tea that Bubbe pours for him.

"I gave Yuri a piece of bread and butter because he said he had a long errand to run for you," Bubbe tells Zayde. Her face is creased with anxiety.

"I have not seen the boy since breakfast! What are you talking about, an errand? I delivered a pair of boots myself to Herr Becker, charged him only half price, and in return, he promised to lend me his cart to take you to the station tomorrow. Yuri must have misunderstood," Zayde says.

Mama picks up Devora, who is pulling at her skirt. She seems to demand more attention these last few days, as if sensing the coming separation. *Can a two-year-old understand that she'll be without her mama, sister, and brother?* I can hardly believe it myself.

"I expect he's playing with Mikhail. After all, it is their last afternoon. I'll run upstairs and fetch him," I say. Anything, rather than watch the look on Mama's face as she holds my sister. My heart begins to pound, as I don't believe for one minute that he is there. The boys have most likely concocted some plan to hide Yuri, goodness knows where. I knock on the Josewitzes' door.

Mikhail's father opens it and asks me inside. "Have you come to say good-bye, Miriam? Well, I wish you all the best. We are going to miss young Yuri around the place."

"Thank you, sir, but we can't find him anywhere. No one has seen him all day!"

Herr Josewitz calls his son, "Mikhail, come here."

Mikhail walks into the room at once, almost as if he has been eavesdropping. He smiles guilelessly at his father. "Do you need me for anything, Papa?"

"Yes." The way his father grabs hold of Mikhail, I think he suspects him of hatching some devious plot with Yuri.

Herr Josewitz says, "Yuri is missing. You must tell his mother where he is immediately. If you are covering up for your friend, think again!"

We all go downstairs together.

Mama speaks gently to Mikhail, but his face remains white. "We are all so worried, Mikhail. You know that we are leaving for America tomorrow. Have you seen Yuri today, or have you any idea where he might be?" she asks him.

Mikhail meets her gaze, and, for a minute, he looks as innocent as Devora. *Is he going to tell the truth?* He and Yuri would rather die than tell tales about each other. For some reason, I think about Malka. I still miss her, so I can understand how the boys would try anything to keep Yuri in Berlin! Mikhail shifts uneasily from one foot to the other.

"I did see Yuri this morning," Mikhail says. "He said he had an errand to run. Then we said good-bye. That is all I can tell you, Aunt Sara."

"I understand that friends must stick together," Mikhail's father says, "but this is serious. If we have to bring in the police, you might both be in more trouble than you can even imagine. I want the truth – do you know where Yuri is or suspect where he might be?"

Mikhail says, "I'm speaking the truth, Father, I don't know where he is. We decided, I mean . . . Yuri said it's better if I don't know his plans. He said that he is going away, a long way away, so that he doesn't have to go to America. We said good-bye and shook hands. That's all. Maybe he's on his way home to Kiev."

"Are you trying to be smart, boy?" Mikhail's father roars.

"No, sir, I'm not." I notice he bites his bottom lip.

Mama says, "Can't you think of somewhere, some hiding place perhaps? It is dark, and we expect more snow. Your father is right, Mikhail. We will have to call in the police."

Kolya comes in. He has taken off his snowy boots, but there are still snowflakes on his jacket. He blows on his fingers. "It's freezing out there. I heard you mention the police. You're not turning me in, are you? If you do, I shall run away to America with you and become a stowaway on the ship," he teases.

Mama buries her face in Devora's hair. She weeps without a sound, but I see her shoulders shake.

"It's not a joke, Kolya. Yuri has run away," Zayde says.

This journey to America is becoming like a bad dream. I almost wish Papa had not sent the tickets!

"Mikhail, where is your favorite place – somewhere you boys enjoy playing?" Kolya asks. Mikhail shrugs and mumbles something about many places. He looks down at the floor, determined not to answer.

I know he knows. Mikhail's father glares at his son.

Suddenly it comes to me – I know where he is! I'm so excited that the words come rushing out. "Mama, I just remembered something. Yuri said he earned money to buy oranges for Devora by working at the stables. He loves that place. It's not too cold in there either. I'm sure that's where he's hiding."

Mikhail's body tenses, but he does not raise his head. *So I'm right!*

As soon as the words are out of my mouth, I realize what I've done. But going to the police would have been worse. I had to tell, and I know Yuri will never forgive me. I've probably broken his heart. It's all I can do to stop myself from apologizing to Mikhail.

Herr Josewitz shouts, "That's it, the stables! I should have guessed. The boys are always finding excuses to be there, ever since they came with me to put in the new window. Mikhail, go to bed. There's no supper for you tonight. I'll deal with you later." The men hurry off.

I'm overcome with guilt. *How could I have given Yuri away, my own brother?* I comfort myself with the knowledge that this is not a game we are playing, that the ship won't wait, trying to excuse what I've done.

Mama, Bubbe, and I stow the food for our journey in a big basket. It seems a lot for just three of us. *Surely, we will get fed on the voyage?* There is a braided challah, a rye loaf and one of black bread, as well as a jar of chicken fat, another of pickled herring, some apples, and honey cake, wrapped up tightly in cloths to keep from drying out. Our bundles, basket, and suitcases are already strapped up. Mama packs Yuri's things.

"They'll find him, Mama. Try not to worry too much," I say.

Mama walks up and down the small kitchen, carrying Devora, who is half asleep. "That boy cannot be trusted for one minute, Miriam," she says. "We will have to watch him every second until the train leaves."

I don't say what I think – that until we actually get him onto the ship, he'll have to be guarded. I wouldn't put it past him to jump off the boat and swim back. Yuri has always been stubborn.

"Let's hope the windows of the train compartment are locked," I say. When I see the look on her face, I add, "I'm only joking, Mama." I feel like slapping Yuri, but I feel sorry for him too. He must be so unhappy to put us through all this.

The runaway is brought back, his cheeks scarlet with cold. I hear Bubbe thanking Mikhail's father, insisting he take a freshly baked challah for his wife.

"Oh, Yuri, how could you worry us so?" Mama says, on the verge of tears.

"I'm sorry, Mama. No one listens to me, I had to. . . ." A tear rolls down his cheek. He wipes his face with his sleeve, and I hand him my handkerchief. His hands are blue.

"Don't you want to see your papa again, Yuri? You know how much he misses us all," Mama says.

"Of course I do, but I want to stay here with Bubbe and Zayde and my friends more. Devora is staying, so why can't I? I've told you and told you how I feel, Mama. Why won't you understand? It's not fair. As for you, Miriam, you are a big sneak, and I am never going to speak to you again." To think I even felt sorry for him a moment ago.

"Enough of that kind of talk, Yuri." Mama has lost her patience with him. "I was ready to go to the police. Miriam, please put Devora in her crib. She is tired."

I do so and place my little doll, the one I have had ever since I was my sister's age, in her arms. I have been saving the doll for this last night. I kept her in my apron pocket all day. She brought back memories of how Malka and I played together, how Malka loved to make little dresses for her doll from bits of cast-off rags. The doll I give to Devora has been a constant reminder of Malka.

Devora clutches the doll. "Mine," she says, beaming at me sleepily.

Yuri is sent to bed without supper, and we eat in silence. What a sad meal, the last but one before our journey. In the morning, it is all we can do to say good-bye to Bubbe. My sister is still fast asleep, and we decide not to wake her. Mama and I cry all the way to the station. Yuri sulks, unspeaking, looking straight ahead.

When the time comes to part from Zayde, after he has unloaded all our belongings and put them on the platform, we just look at each other for a long moment. Mama keeps tight hold of Yuri's wrist, so that he does not get back in the cart or dash away somewhere. She manages a smile.

"Soon," Mama says, "soon we will all be together again. Take care of yourselves and of my little girl, Father." He puts his hand on our heads, briefly, and his lips move in a blessing before he turns away.

9

ALONE

We wave to Zayde long after he is out of sight. The arrival of the train forces us to turn towards it. Now our journey can really begin. I am the first one to clamber up the steps, so that Mama and Yuri can hand the luggage up to me. After putting down the first bundle, I discover that Yuri has gone. *What now?* Other travelers climb onto the train, loaded down with their belongings.

"Mama, where is Yuri?" I scream. At that moment, I notice his brown cap disappearing behind a luggage cart. "Over there, Mama, quick!" I rush down the steps, and we run after him.

A guard appears. "The train will depart shortly, ladies."

"Yes, sir." I smile at him, drag Yuri out, and hand him over to Mama.

"March," she says and stands close behind Yuri as he climbs the steps, deliberately slowly. We struggle with our belongings and find our seats. Yuri is wedged beside the window, I'm next to him, and Mama collapses on the aisle seat as the train lurches forward with a great hiss of steam. The other passengers look as if they have been settled for a while. There is an old woman wearing a kerchief, sleeping with her mouth open, who snores a little. Next to her, a small girl devours a piece of black bread. Her mother tells her not to gobble it so fast.

We are going such a long way, away from Devora, Bubbe, and Zayde. *Will we have to wait two years until we see them again?* That's how long we were without Papa. As the train wheels go round and round, they seem to echo my thoughts, *far away, far away.* I wonder if the wheels chant in Russian or Yiddish or German or all three, depending on where the passenger comes from. I look at the German-English dictionary that Kolya gave me for my birthday. It is small enough to fit in my pocket. He wrote in it: *To Miriam, an excellent pupil, from your friend, Kolya.* I shall miss him – he has become like an older brother to us.

Yuri can't be angry with me forever. His eyes are shut, but I think he is only pretending to be asleep. I can tell by the way his eyelids flutter that he is awake.

"Yuri," I whisper, "please forgive me for giving your hiding place away. We were so worried about you!" He pretends not to hear me. He has not spoken a word since last night.

The woman opposite us wipes tears from her eyes. Mama pours a beaker of tea from the flask we brought and offers it to her. "Have you come far?" she asks the woman.

"Thank you. Yes, we changed trains in Danzig. Before that, we came from Grodno. So many stops, so many questions they ask, those doctors and inspectors. The disinfecting, the scrubbing and prodding, making us feel like animals. In Hamburg, it will be the same thing, and if they don't like the answer or think we are unfit, 'undesirables' as they call us, then they will turn us back." I sense Yuri is listening. He shifts slightly in his seat.

The woman continues, "It is the new regulations. The steamship companies don't want to pay for people who are sent back from New York. The Golden Land is only for the healthy and smart." She wipes the beaker on her skirt and returns it, thanking Mama. The woman seems happy to have a good listener. "I hear you will have fewer problems, coming from Germany. For us . . . straight from Russia, I don't know. What are they afraid of? That we carry some plague?" She sighs deeply, as though bewildered at all that has happened to her.

Mother tells her about Devora, about having to leave her behind.

"I am sorry for you," the woman says, "but think how lucky you are to have family to take care of her until she is well. You want to know something? I am afraid. I have not seen my husband and son for four years. How much will they have changed? The old one," she points to her sleeping mother, "how will she like it over there? Can she learn a new language?"

I stop listening because I have noticed Yuri's face. The sullen look has been replaced by his usual mischievous one. He's up to something, but what?

Please, Yuri, don't cause any more problems. Haven't we waited long enough to see Papa again? Even if he could read my thoughts, in his present mood, he'd ignore them.

The train slows down and the guard calls out, "Hamburg." The engine has hardly come to a halt before people scramble out onto the platform. Everyone is in a hurry to get their luggage out safely, to be first in line to wherever we are supposed to go. Small children peer down onto the gleaming rails under the train and are dragged off, protesting, by their mothers.

Mama tells me to count our pieces of luggage. She has not let go of Yuri for a second, holding on to the back of his jacket or a sleeve as we are jostled by the crowd. He looks pale, with big circles under his eyes. She relents, gently brushing the hair from his eyes. Whistles blow. Men speaking in Yiddish accost travelers, offering to exchange money or sell tickets.

One grabs the ends of my shawl. "You need nice clean room, miss?" I shudder away. Mama pushes at him with her basket.

"Go away, or I'll call the police," she says. Thankfully, the scrawny man has already turned to accost someone else.

"How often do I have to tell you, Miriam," Mama says, "if a strange man speaks to you, look away. Never answer anyone, unless he is a policeman or wearing an official uniform. Girls disappear as quickly as this." She snaps her fingers together. "There are bad people here. Now stay close to me, both of you."

It would be useless to tell her I did not say a single word to him or that white slavers would not dare to lure me away with Mama watching! I've heard stories of girls enticed away, by the offer of a place to stay or a good job, and never heard from again! Mama is forever warning me about strangers.

She starts again, "Especially at railway stations and when disembarking from a ship. Bad people know one is alone, bewildered, ready to believe anything, flattered by a nice smile."

We follow the crowd leaving the station, led by two uniformed men telling us to be quick. There are hundreds and hundreds of us. *How will they make room for us all on the ship?*

"Where are we going now, do you think, Mama?" I ask.

A tall girl wearing a bright red shawl, her hair hanging in a long dark braid down her back, turns around to speak to us. "To the Hamburg emigration building," she says. She is not walking with anyone. *Is she all by herself?* She does not look much older than me.

I can smell the River Elbe. I point to the ships in the harbor. "Look, Yuri, one of those ships might be the one taking us to America." He pretends not to hear me. I'm getting tired of his silly game. *Why doesn't Mama put her foot down?* We are nudged and pushed up several steps into a large gray building. Voices in several languages tell steerage passengers to hurry up and proceed to the passenger halls. Officials surround us, demanding to look at our papers, asking where we are from. Interpreters translate. Then we are divided into roped-off lines – one is for those who have traveled from Russia, ours is for those who have traveled from within Germany, and another is for people from other countries in Europe.

I wave good-bye to the little girl who was on the train with us. It doesn't seem fair that her family has to go through all the things they have already experienced along the way, again. The girl with the red shawl has moved several places ahead of us.

Some people are arguing with the officers, saying they have papers for America, asking why they are being treated differently than travelers from Germany. One of the uniformed men explains they must go to the quarantine barracks first, for questioning and disinfecting, before they can proceed. Our line moves forward. My arms are already tired from carrying my luggage. There are several inspectors ahead, who will look through our things. Luckily all our belongings get stamped as INSPECTED, a red label fastened to each item, a yellow one to say DISINFECTED.

Just when I think we are finished, we find out that we must be examined by the emigration doctor. In single file, we pass in front of a stern-looking man in a white coat. A nurse stands beside him, as well as a uniformed man who writes in a little notebook. The nurse checks our names against our luggage labels and writes them down on a list. She tells us our tickets must be stamped by the US consulate in Hamburg. The man who is writing in a notebook must be from the US consulate. I just hope that Yuri will be on his very best behavior and answers all the doctor's questions nicely.

I go first and give my name and age before the doctor looks in my ears and mouth. He listens to my chest and asks me to cough, then to read some numbers from a chart on the wall behind him. I read out a sentence written on a grubby card. Then the nurse hands him something that looks like a black buttonhook. He turns back my eyelid. I can't help wincing, gasping with the shock and pain of it.

My ticket is stamped, and the nurse smiles at me. I've passed! While Mama is asked some more questions, I am told to wait by the exit. She joins me in a few minutes, and we wait anxiously for Yuri's ticket to be stamped too.

The doctor asks Yuri his name. His face is blank, and his lips are clamped shut. When they ask him his age, an interpreter repeats both questions. Nothing is forthcoming. Mama is about to step forward, but I hold her back. The doctor takes Yuri by the chin and forces his mouth open, then he looks in his ears. After he has listened to his chest, he walks behind my brother. Suddenly the doctor claps his hands together sharply. The noise startles me, even though I have been expecting it. Yuri does not move.

"Look at me!" the doctor shouts. There is no response. Mama rushes forward and grabs hold of Yuri. *Does she think she can shake the words out of him?* I can tell he will not let himself be persuaded to speak. We all overheard the woman on the train who said the "unfit" are turned back. Yuri has decided to imitate Kolya's brother, Lev, who did not speak.

Mama says, "You must stop this nonsense, Yuri. It is not a game. It is your life, all our lives. Answer the doctor, I beg you, my son."

The doctor is tapping the table impatiently, with a pointer. She turns to him.

"Sir," Mama says, "Yuri is a normal intelligent boy, just shy and afraid."

The doctor ignores Mama's protests.

"He is rejected. Your son is defective. The boy will be sent back tomorrow. Arrangements will be made for his safe return. Next."

My brain cannot take in his words. *Defective? Impossible!* My brother has an answer for everything. He can recognize any military regiment just by looking at the buttons on the uniform.

Mama slaps Yuri hard, once on each cheek. "Speak, you stubborn boy! Don't do this," she says.

An officer pulls Mama away and points us to the door. I cannot see Yuri's face, but the way he stands and his narrow bony shoulders are still those of a little boy. Perhaps he has earned the right to stay awhile longer. Perhaps I can make amends for giving his hiding place away.

"Mama, please let him be. He can't help it, he is so unhappy. Bubbe and Zayde will take care of him. He can come with them later." Still Yuri does not move, but I think I see some of the stiffness go out of the shoulders he has held rigidly for so long. "I beg you, Mama, come now. We have to go. Look, our tickets are stamped – the ship will leave without us." I pick up the basket of food and my things. Mama looks from Yuri to me, her face ashen. With tears rolling down her cheeks, she walks towards Yuri and takes his hand in hers. An awful thought comes to me. I have to hold myself back from throwing myself into my mother's arms.

"Miriam, you will have to go without me," Mama says. "I cannot leave both Devora and Yuri without a mother. Tell Papa I will come later." She turns to go.

I stare at Mama. *She is not coming!* I cry out, "What about me, Mama? Don't Papa and I matter? What of the tickets, wasted?"

"I have no choice, Miriam," Mama says. "You are a strong young woman; you will manage." She stifles a sob. "Be well, my child. I will keep you in my prayers. Tell Sam I will come." There is no more time to beg, to plead, and to tell her how much I need her.

The officer opens the door and points to the line of people. He says the tender is waiting to take me to the ship. Mama and Yuri have disappeared. I almost wish that I had not passed, that I had gone back with them. Then the thought of Papa, who has worked and waited so long for us, makes me strong.

I am going to America, to be with Papa again. Only, I wish, I wish, I was not so alone.

The Atlantic Ocean, February 1910

10

JOURNEY TO THE "GOLDEN LAND"

An officer checks my ticket and points to a line of people that slowly winds its way out of the building. The tenders are waiting outside on the quay. I ask the woman in front of me, holding a child by each hand, if she knows what is happening.

She looks me up and down and says, "What do you think, silly girl? We get on board, we sail, what else?" She turns back to her children. I feel foolish and ignorant.

We reach one of the tenders that will take us to the ship. Officers count us and check our tickets again. I know I cannot be the only girl traveling alone, but if anyone asks me if I am by myself, I will burst into tears. I look for a seat and am told to hurry up and sit down. Never a smile or a "welcome aboard," nothing to reassure us about the unknown.

An arm beckons, a flash of scarlet. A voice calls out, "Over here, there is room beside me." It is the girl who was ahead of us in the line earlier, the one wearing the red shawl. Thankfully I take my place beside her, put my bundle on my case, and rest my feet on top. The picnic basket is balanced on my lap. I notice a man in a white coat going up to passengers, telling them to roll up their sleeves. The children wail at the sight of a big needle.

The girl says, "That's the ship's doctor. He is vaccinating us, so we do not spread disease on the ship. They are afraid of typhoid. We might have picked up anything from all those crowds. It'll soon be over," she says with a friendly smile. I thank her, but my thoughts are with Mama and Yuri. I won't cry.

Yuri has got what he wanted for now, but what is to become of him next time? Now that his name is on the list as rejected, will he even be admitted to America with the others? Mama will have to sort it out. I am too tired to worry anymore.

It is good to sit down – we seem to have been standing and waiting for hours. The boat is full, and we set off. Another tender is behind us and another one after that. So many emigrants, all going to the Golden Land, and my stubborn brother, whom I love despite everything, is left behind. Worse, Mama has chosen to stay with him. *How am I going to tell Papa?* She will have to write to explain it to him, and, hopefully, the letter will reach America before I arrive.

The girl beside me says, "My name is Rosina Brunetti. I am from Italy. I have been working for a well-to-do family in Hamburg for two years, since I was thirteen, looking after their three children and doing housework. This is where I learned to speak German. Now I have saved enough to go and live with my older brother. I have not met his wife yet. They married in America, but she is Italian, like us, so I am not worried. I will find work, pay for my keep, and send money home, and one day the rest of the family can join us. What about you? Where are your mother and the boy? Are they on the next tender?" she asks. I burst into tears.

Rosina puts her hand on my arm. "Don't cry, little one. Did they send them to quarantine?" I shake my head, unable to speak.

"Many are returned – if they have the eye disease or sickness of the lungs. Sometimes they are kept in quarantine, until they are cured. They can try again later, you will see. Do you go to relatives?"

I manage to answer her. "Yes, to my father. What will he say when he sees I am the only one coming, after he worked so hard to send us tickets?" Then I tell this kind Italian girl everything that has happened, about Devora and Yuri and the doctor's words. I can hardly bear to repeat them.

"Yuri is 'defective,' he said." I explain Mama's decision to return with Yuri to Berlin. When I speak about this, it seems cruel that Mama sent me to cross the ocean by myself. *Does it mean she loves the others more than me?* I know that's not true. Mama had to choose, that's all, and they are younger and need her most.

I do not usually talk about family matters to strangers. There must be something about a journey that makes us want to confide secrets to people we hardly know. It was the same on the train to Hamburg, when Mama spoke so openly to the woman from Russia.

Rosina is outraged on our behalf. "That doctor has no heart. What a cruel man to speak to you like this. Your poor mama could not let your little brother go back alone – impossible! She must have been worried and sad to leave her little daughter too. Tell me your name," she says. I wipe my eyes.

"My name is Miriam Markov. It used to be Markowitz, before they changed Papa's name on Ellis Island," I say, feeling a little better.

"I am alone too, Miriam, so let us help each other on the journey, and then we will not be alone anymore, yes?" She holds out her hand and we shake, sealing our friendship.

"My friends call me Rosie," she says.

"I like that," I try it out. "Rosie . . . I am so glad we met."

Suddenly, Rosie starts to laugh. She says, "He is a smart boy, your brother, don't you think, fooling the *dottore?*"

I have to agree. "Yes, I'm quite proud of him." *Who but my brother would want to be sent back, when it is the dream of every Jew I've ever heard of to go to the Golden Land?* Rosie smiles at me.

It is time to stop feeling sorry for myself. Everything will turn out all right. I'm on my way to America! I'll make Mama and Papa proud of me.

"I am a year younger than you, Rosie, but that's old enough to travel and find work in America. Now that we've met, I'm not scared anymore. I think we might even enjoy ourselves. It is a big adventure, isn't it? Are you hungry? I have tea and bread and . . ." I raise the lid of my basket and show Rosie the good things Bubbe packed for us. "Please help yourself."

She takes an apple, and I cut two thick slices of challah, one for each for us. Bubbe even wrapped up a knife. She has thought of everything.

Rosie thanks me. "This is the Jewish bread, Miriam? I have never tried it before – it's delicious. My mama and papa and three little brothers are still in Italy, in Napoli. Papa worked in a bakery all his life, since a small boy, but he got sick and was laid off. Who knows when they will be able to come to America. I will work hard and send money to help them."

The woman next to me rocks her baby, who hasn't stopped crying since we left Hamburg. Someone says we will soon arrive in Cuxhaven, where we will board our ship. Rosie found out that the other passengers, from the second- and first-class cabins, come by train.

The motion of the boat makes me sleepy, and I doze off until I hear those familiar words: "Hurry up." Rosie shakes my shoulder. For a moment, I don't know where I am. *What does she want?* I cannot have slept all the way to America. I look up at the huge ship towering over us and read the name on the side, SS *Amerika*.

Officials herd us up a gangway and check our tickets and luggage. Then we are on board! An officer points us towards a twisting staircase that leads down to the lowest deck, where we will spend the next fourteen days. There is no time to look at anything. Rosie is behind me and warns me not to fall.

The stairs are very narrow and seem to go down forever. I have trouble managing my belongings. People jostle, trying to calm excited or fretful children. Some women are sobbing because they have been separated from their husbands, sons, or fathers. I turn my head to look for Rosie, but now there are several women between us. I have lost sight of her. I drag my suitcase with one hand, my other holds the basket, and my bundle is somehow wedged under the same arm. I am in front of an impatient woman who deliberately pushes me.

"I'm moving as fast as I can," I say, turning my head to look at her. She is huge and wears numerous shawls over her bulky frame. I feel dizzy from trying to keep upright and prevent my possessions from slipping away from me.

"Go on, you're holding us all up," she says, poking me with the corner of her case. She tries to get past me on the stairs. *Why is she in such a hurry?* The ship won't leave till all the passengers are settled. I catch my heel on the slippery iron step, but even without a hand free to grip the railing, I manage to stumble on into the darkness without falling. Once down, it is like landing in a cold dark pit.

A steward in a white coat stands at the bottom of the stairs, which I thought would never end. He points towards the long, narrow, dark corridor, which he calls an alleyway, to find our berths.

I pause for a moment to catch my breath and wish I hadn't, for the air is foul and damp, smelling of bodies, sweat, and fear. Mixed in are the odors of grease, wet wool, and oil. We are deep in the hold of the ship, close to the engines. Something runs over my foot. *Is it a rat?* Of course I've seen rats before, skittering over the cobbles in the Barn Quarter, beady eyes staring out from under pushcarts, but this close? Ugh, it is all I can do not to scream!

The steward orders us to move along. I suppose the men's cabins are at the other end of the ship. I've never been on a liner before and have no idea how things are arranged. I'll make sure I find out, the way I always do. I'm not afraid of pogroms or fire here, but I need to know what to do if something bad happens. The first chance I get, I will go up on deck and find out where the lifeboats are.

This is not the time to think about danger. Everyone on board has been saving and waiting for this moment. What is important is to remember how lucky I am to be going to my papa. As I walk past rows of little rooms like train compartments, peering through the narrow open doors of each one, I look for berths for Rosie and me. So far, they are already occupied by women and girls of every shape and size, speaking in Yiddish, Polish, German, Italian, and Russian. There seem to be four wooden tiers of bunks on each side and not much space in between. *Wherever are we going to keep our luggage?* The first ten cabins are already full or have only one empty bunk left. Rosie and I decided to try for two top berths, so that we'll be more private. We'll be the ones climbing over other passengers, not the other way around. I smile, thinking of the fat lady trying to climb up onto the narrow berth.

I'm out of luck – the next three cabins are full too. I've just about given up hope of finding two upper berths, when I discover the next cabin is still unoccupied. Slipping on the greasy floor, I almost fall again in my eagerness to claim our berths.

I throw my bundle on the top bunk and my shawl on the one opposite, to save it for Rosie. Then I hoist my suitcase and picnic basket up the little set of steps. I look down and see a woman settling her little girl on the bottom berth.

At that moment, Rosie hurries in and leans against the

bunk post. She is out of breath, as if she's been running. For a moment, I wonder if we're on the wrong ship or if something has happened for her to look so anxious. I realize that I already look on Rosie as a friend, the first girlfriend I've made since Malka disappeared.

II

STEERAGE

"I tried to catch up with you, Miriam," Rosie says, "but, every time, someone pushed between us! I was worried about losing you. You have got us top bunks – *perfetto*, how you say? Perfect! A window would be nice, but you can't have everything." She climbs up and surveys our new home, then starts to unpack. Others come in – two young women, sisters or friends, one pale with dark shadows under her eyes and her stomach bulging out under her shawl. She is brave to travel when she's expecting a baby.

The other woman helps her onto the bunk. "Rest, Anna," she says. "I'm going to be right above you. I'll unpack in a minute. Let me help you take off your boots. You're supposed to keep your feet up. Don't argue – you need to lie down for a while." She's bossy, so I'm sure they are sisters!

Each bunk has a straw mattress covered in blue checked gingham, and the pillow is filled with seaweed. I smell it. This is the first scent of the sea I have experienced since coming aboard. There is a thin woolen blanket, but I brought an extra shawl and another blanket, in case it gets cold.

The small cabin soon fills up. We introduce ourselves. We are going to be sharing this small windowless space for many days at sea, so we need to know a bit about each other. I hope we get along. I don't expect everyone to be as nice as Rosie. We are so lucky to have found each other!

I try to remember all the names. Fanny is the mother of little Essie, who is four. They share one bunk. She says she is meeting her husband in New York and that they have been separated for three years. She is from Danzig, and before that, from Bialystok.

"I talk to Essie about her papa," Fanny says. "She doesn't really remember him, I'm afraid. He writes that he has been working in a butcher's shop, on Hester Street. It is hard to picture these strange streets and the new life he leads," she says.

Anna tells us that she and her sister, Eva, are traveling with their husbands. They hope they will be able to meet on the boat, perhaps on deck. They are all garment workers and plan to find an apartment and work from there. They would have liked to have a family cabin, but it is cheaper for the men to travel dormitory-style. They have come from Vienna, Austria. There are so many nationalities on this one ship, yet America welcomes us all!

The confidences start almost at once. As we unpack, we share our hopes. We are human beings with names, not numbers waiting in line to be called, counted, questioned, hurried on, or sent back. We are alike because we are emigrants, but different too, each with her own story.

Two girls, looking a year or so older than Rosie, have just come in. They collapse with exhaustion, filling the floor space with their mounds of luggage. Now only one bunk is left. I doubt that it will stay empty for long. The ship is going to stop one more time, at Cherbourg, to take on more passengers.

The girls brighten up as they shed their belongings. "I'm Tanya," one says, "and this is my cousin, Riva. We are not married yet," she says with a giggle.

Riva says, "We come from Grodno, Russia, and hope to find rich American husbands! My brother has found me a place as an assistant cook in a big private house, where he is a chauffeur. He has been in America for four years."

Tanya says, "I will be a nursemaid, with the same family. We will be on trial for three months. I have seven younger brothers and sisters, so I've got lots of experience."

We are busy trying to accommodate not only ourselves, but our luggage. For once, I'm glad I'm not very tall. It means there is room at the end of the bunk for my suitcase. Kolya's feet would hang over the edge!

Oh, how I miss everyone and wonder what they are doing at this moment. *Are Mama and Yuri still on the train or waiting at the station to catch one in the morning?* If Yuri had come with us, he would have had to sleep in a dormitory with the men, and Mama would have been worrying about him every single minute. Sometimes things do happen for the best. Who knows, in a year, with me helping to earn money and Devora older and stronger, we might all be together again.

We try to squeeze our belongings under and on our bunks, leaving the passageway clear between the bunks. Once the single overhead bulb goes out, it would be easy to fall over anything left in the way.

How lucky I am. There is a nail, hammered loosely in the wooden partition that separates our cabin from the one next door. I can hear every sound through the thin wall. I hang up my shawl and spare skirt. Rosie is desperately looking for a nail too, but hasn't found one, so I offer to hang up her skirt over mine. I spread my shawl over my feet.

A large figure looms in the doorway. A woman enters. I recognize her immediately. Her presence and demanding voice seem to take up whatever small space there is.

"Good, you've got room in here. I need a bottom bunk. Do you mind taking the middle one opposite, so I can have yours?" the woman asks Anna. *What nerve!*

Eva answers quickly, "I'm afraid that is not possible. My sister is going to have a baby. This is the easiest bunk for her to climb in and out of. Please take your case off her bed."

The woman turns to Essie's mother. "What about you then, missus?" Fanny hesitates. *Will she refuse?* I hope she does.

Fanny searches for the right words. "Well, I would, but I've just settled the child," she says. "I'm sure there is room farther on. I'm sorry." Without another word, the woman leaves. I'm just telling the others how she treated me on the stairs and what a lucky escape we've had, when the last berth is taken. A woman, who reminds me of a school teacher I had when I was a little girl in Kiev, has come in. She terrified me, rapping my knuckles for the smallest fault.

She is tall, thin, and stern looking. She says her name is Pearl Kurtz, and she is from Minsk, in Russia, where she kept house for her brother, with whom she is traveling. *Does she ever smile?*

"Where is the porthole?" she asks.

Porthole – is there is a hole in the ship? I don't know what she's talking about.

She stares at our blank faces. "The window. I must have fresh air," she says.

"The windows are in second class, ma'am, this is steerage. Are you sure your ticket is for steerage?" Riva says, barely able to keep from laughing.

Pearl takes no notice of her, picks up her pillow, sniffs, turns, and examines the mattress. Grudgingly, she says, "Better than nothing, I suppose. My idiot of a brother is going to work on a chicken farm in the Catskills. I'm forced to accompany him; there is no one else. I had better get used to hardship. This is a fool's journey, I'm sure." She starts to unpack, merely nodding her head in acknowledgment when we introduce ourselves. "I hope no one snores, I'm a poor sleeper," Pearl announces. No one says anything.

Rosie whispers, "Come outside. Let's look for the washroom before the crowds gather."

Mama had reminded me that no towel would be provided. Mine is at the top of my bundle. We find the washroom along the corridor. There are only six toilets between hundreds of women, and each one is in the narrowest of cubicles. Rosie and I are so disgusted, we can barely look at each other.

"An open trough and that high iron step – I've never used anything like this. Where I worked in Hamburg, there was a flush toilet. I didn't expect anything grand, but this is awful," Rosie says.

We wash under one of the cold-water faucets, one for each of the ten basins – five on each side of the wall. Several women are there already. One wipes her little girl's face, and the child puts out her tongue to lick the water.

"Mama, it tastes of salt!" Her mother explains to her that the water comes straight from the sea. Bubbe would say salt is healthy!

We wash as best we can, hurrying to make way for the line of women waiting for us to finish. There are no cloths to clean the basins. *How are so many of us going to wash and do our laundry?* Ten basins are not very many. Next time, I'm going to bring a rag to wipe the basin before I use it, even if I have to tear it from my petticoat!

"Can you imagine what this place is going to look and smell like after a few days at sea?" Rosie says.

"I'd rather not, Rosie. In his first letter to us, Papa hinted about steerage conditions on board. I didn't expect much, but this is pretty horrible. I am glad Mama and Devora are not here. Papa and I will have to save up more, so that they can travel second-class. Oh, my goodness, just listen to me! If my grandmother were here, she'd say, 'Who do you think you are, a rich American lady, already?'"

"Come on, let's get out of here and explore a bit. *Mamma mia*, Miriam, the ship is moving." Rosie grabs my arm. "The floor is sliding away from us." Engines clatter and jangle, and the ship sways, tilting from one side to the other. We are on our way to the other side of the world!

A bell rings, and I almost collide with the steward, who calls out that supper is being served in the dining room.

"Go all the way along the alleyway, straight ahead," he says.

I am surprised. I don't really know what I was expecting
– that we'd line up along the corridor, I mean alleyway, and
pass bowls of food along from hand to hand?

When we get to the dining room, we see long wooden
tables and benches set up in rows. A knife, fork, and spoon
and a bowl and mug are laid for each person. On the tables
are baskets of fresh white bread, dishes of jam, and jugs
of cocoa. The stewards bring big tin pots filled with potato
and vegetable stew. It is a welcome meal, the first for many
hours. We help ourselves and eat as fast as possible, taking
our empty plates to a side table, so that clean utensils can be
set for the women waiting their turn. There are too many of
us to be fed at one sitting. Women with children are served
first, but Fanny noticed us and took Essie on her knee, so
that we could squeeze in beside her.

We take a long time settling down after supper. The cabin is
small, and it is hard for all of us to sort our belongings and
get into our bunks. My arm throbs, and there is a red bump
where the doctor injected the needle. The engines grind,
and the noise is so close to my ear that, even on the top
bunk, I feel as if I am resting right on top of the machinery.
Next door, a baby wails. I am too excited to go to sleep. The
lightbulb dims.

Rosie and I whisper about our plans for tomorrow. We
are going to go up on deck as soon as breakfast is over.

Pearl's voice interrupts us, "Are you planning to talk all night? I need my sleep."

I don't know why, but she makes me want to laugh. I try to stifle my giggles in my pillow.

"Don't, you'll suffocate in the seaweed," Rosie whispers, and that starts me off again.

Pearl sits up. She sounds exactly like my old teacher. "I warn you, girls, I'll call the steward if you don't stop talking!"

"Shame on you, Pearl," Tanya says, "inviting men into the women's quarters."

Now everyone is laughing, except for her. But, ten minutes later, when she begins to snore, Riva shakes her by the shoulder and tells her to be quiet. Magically, Pearl is silent from then on!

12

"WRETCHED REFUSE"

This morning, there is no laughter. Anna, Essie, and I are the only ones who manage to get up. The others moan in agonies of seasickness. I help Essie to fasten the buttons on her dress. Then the three of us make our way down the alleyway, hearing pitiful wails from the cabins. We join a line of pale-faced women, waiting to use the washroom.

Walking to the dining room, I feel the ship toss and sway. I am amazed that, even though I feel a bit off balance, I am perfectly well and very hungry again!

"How long will the ship bounce and rock?" Anna asks the steward.

He laughs. "This is nothing. We are on the Atlantic Ocean, and conditions are good. You have to expect the open sea to be a bit choppy at this time of year. There is bound to be much worse weather before we arrive."

The dining room is almost empty. We help ourselves to porridge, bread and butter, apples, and tea. I put two apples in my pocket, one each for Rosie and Fanny. Anna eats heartily, and so do I. She pats her stomach.

"At home, I felt sick every morning, but now I'm fine," she says. "I think the baby likes the rocking of the ship."

Before we return to the cabin, I ask one of the dining room stewards if I may please take some tea up to my friend and to the little girl's mother. Anna begs for some too, for her sister. He sighs impatiently and is about to refuse us, but Essie puts her hands together and smiles up at him.

"Please?" she whispers.

"We can't be bringing tea to the passengers, not in steerage," the steward says gruffly.

"Please, sir, just this once – won't you make an exception?" I ask.

The steward softens. He goes off into the galley and comes back with a jug of tea and some mugs. "Don't make a habit of asking for favors," he says, turning away before we can thank him.

Anna persuades her sister and Fanny to swallow a bit of the tea, and I do my best with Rosie.

"Leave me alone – I want to die! Why did I ever leave Hamburg?" Rosie cries.

I encourage her to swallow a few sips, and she actually

manages to keep the tea down. Then I help her from her bunk and out of our cramped quarters. We kept our clothes on last night because we were so cold. Rosie hangs on to my arm for balance. She is trembling, and her face is ghostly white. I repeat what the steward said, that this is normal weather.

"I expect you feel sick, Rosie, because it's your first time on a liner. The train we were on was worse than this, the way it stopped, started, and jolted. We just have to move with the boat. Breathe deeply once we're on deck, and don't look at the water. Look at the horizon." I sound like Bubbe. I can't think where I got this advice from. Rosie nods bravely, determined to try.

"Let me wrap your shawl round you. Now, just a few steps up the stairs, and we will be on deck. You will feel heaps better soon." The steps are slick with seawater, but we succeed in climbing up and onto the open deck.

It is magnificent out here, with nothing to look at but waves, churning and foaming, as the ship parts the ocean. The sky above us seems to go on forever. It changes constantly, clouds making pictures over our heads.

There are only a few men and women outside – relatives seeking each other out, I imagine. It is very cold, but a different cold from the cabin. Here, the wind blows fresh and clean, gusts whip our skirts, and we have difficulty holding them down.

I find a sheltered spot under an overhanging lifeboat. There are no seats anywhere, and we huddle together on the wooden boards of the deck. This is the lowest deck, the only one steerage passengers may use. I take an apple out of my pocket, grateful for the knife Bubbe packed for me. I slice the apple thinly and feed Rosie as if she were Devora. She is able to keep a few slices down.

To take her mind off her nausea, I pull out my dictionary and read the lines of the poem that Kolya copied down for me. It is called "The New Colossus," by Emma Lazarus, New York, 1883. Next to the original poem, he has translated each English word into German, to make it easier for me to understand.

"Who is this Kolya?" Rosie asks. "Why have you not mentioned him before?"

I tell her, "Kolya escaped from the police, when he was studying at the University of Vilna. In Berlin, he is an apprentice in a publishing house. Kolya knows all kinds of things about books and manuscripts. He speaks several languages.

"He has been teaching English to my family for two years and boards with us since Papa left." I realize how much I am going to miss him in America.

We read and discuss the poem, which is about the Statue of Liberty. The poet calls her the "Mother of Exiles" because she welcomes rich and poor alike to America. The poem,

Kolya writes, is engraved on a plaque inside the pedestal on which the statue stands. Together, Rosie and I try reading some of the English words aloud:

> *"Give me your tired, your poor,*
> *Your huddled masses yearning to breathe free,*
> *The wretched refuse of your teeming shore.*
> *Send these, the homeless, tempest-tossed to me,*
> *I lift my lamp beside the golden door!"*

"That's what I am, how you say? 'Tempest-tossed,'" Rosie says.

"We are not homeless, are we, Rosie? Let's exchange addresses, so that we will never lose each other."

Rosie's brother lives on Cherry Street, where she says many Italian families have settled. I hope Clinton Street is not far away from her, so we can visit each other.

We are alone on deck now. It is too cold and windy to stay here any longer.

As we walk along the alleyway, back to our cabin, Rosie nudges me. "That sailor is loitering outside the washrooms again," she whispers. "I noticed him last night, trying to catch sight of a pair of ankles. He's got no business down here – these are women's quarters. He's not the one who rings the bell for meals. Up to no good, I bet. Be careful – don't give him even a glance."

"Oh, Rosie, you are as bad as Mama. She thinks every man is a kidnapper," I say.

"I'm serious, Miriam," Rosie says, "no one would hear if . . . well if anything happened, so let's stick together. I know you like to wander the ship, but try to wait till I'm with you."

"I'll do my best," I say, laughing at her.

The days and nights pass slowly, but at the end of our first week on board, a violent storm shakes us awake. The ship plunges and rears, and little Essie rolls out of the bunk she shares with her mother. We are terrified. The vessel creaks and groans; the machinery beneath us grinds, clatters, and rasps. The moans and cries from cabins on either side of us, and from our own, seem to signal the end of the world.

I stumble, heaving, shaking, to the washroom, joining scores of girls and women. The thought of going back to our fetid cabin is dreadful. Instead, I drag myself in almost total darkness to the stairs, craving just one breath of air. The floor around the bottom of the steps leading to the deck is ankle-deep in water. My skirt hem is soaked. I climb the stairs, grateful for a gulp of air at the top. The wind almost blows me over. A sailor shouts at me to go down again, before I'm washed overboard. I do as I'm told, unsure if I'm awake or having a nightmare. All along the alleyway, wretched women and children are crying hopelessly and vomiting.

No one comes down to help us clean up, to bring a little tea or water, a word of comfort. "Wretched refuse," Emma Lazarus calls us, and that is how we are treated. Somehow I crawl back up to my bunk.

The hours pass. I can't tell day from night. I close my eyes and dream that Mama is here. She places a cool cloth on my forehead. Washes me with sweet-smelling soap, changes my gown. Mama lifts a glass of water to my cracked lips. I thank her and hold out my arms, but she is not there. I want my mother. I want to go home.

I grip the side of my bunk, afraid to roll off. The overhead bulb dims and brightens or goes out, swaying with the movement of the ship. It is as if a giant is toying with us. *Will he get tired of us? Will we drown before we reach the Golden Land?*

The storm lasts all the next day and night. Listening to the foghorn's eerie warning, I think that nothing can ever happen to me worse than this. I could hide from the pogrom, but I can't hide from the storm.

On the second night, there is a scream so piercing and tragic that Rosie and I manage to raise our heads. Later, I wish that I had slithered down from my bunk to help, but that was after we found out what had caused that agonizing cry.

We wake up to calm seas. For the first time in days, passengers crowd the dining room for breakfast. When we go up on deck, everything smells fresh and clean, unlike below.

A small group of men and women stand protectively around a grief-stricken mother. Her baby son died in the night. He has already been buried at sea. We hear that a rabbi spoke a kaddish for the baby. His father was not there to say the prayer for the dead. The mother's friends do their best to console her. Two little girls cling to her skirts. How I pity the mother, losing her baby and having to break such news to her husband when she arrives in America. It must have been her scream we heard in the night. . . .

Whenever the weather permits, the deck is busy: groups of men play cards, others play the harmonica. Girls sing, a few even dance. Women make friends and gossip with each other. Families walk round the deck, and children shout and play freely. I can't help thinking Yuri should be playing chase round the deck, clambering on the railings with the other boys, enjoying the freedom and fresh sea air.

In a short while, we will arrive. Rosie and I teach each other words in English and Italian. Today, for the first time, even Pearl is talking with a group of older women. This is unusual for her. She likes to keep to herself or lies in wait for her brother, no doubt to make him miserable with her nagging.

Tonight, after our meager supper, which gets worse each day, I share the last of Bubbe's honey cake with our cabin mates. Even her black bread, when dipped in salt water to soften, is not that bad. We have hardly seen more than a cupful of fresh water for days, and the milk is only for the youngest children.

We get ready for bed, talking over the day's events. Pearl is the last one to return to the cabin, bursting to share some gossip she's picked up on deck. Full of her own importance, she asks us if we've heard what happened to the Polish girl in the cabin three doors down from us. We don't give her any encouragement, guessing it's something unpleasant.

"Let this be a lesson to girls who are too friendly with the crew," she says. "No one knows if the girl arranged to meet the sailor or if he just happened to be there and she encouraged him with her fancy ways. . . . She was almost raped, I hear. Her blouse was torn and . . ." She pauses dramatically. Essie is listening with the rest of us, her eyes wide. Fanny puts her hands over the child's ears.

"If her mother had not come looking for her, wondering why she was so long returning to her cabin, and dragged her away, who knows what might have occurred. Of course, it's not for me to say, but I hear she encouraged him. That girl is always showing herself off, flouncing around, making eyes at the men on deck, smiling at the stewards and crew. No wonder one of them thought his attentions would be welcome."

"You are just spreading rumors," I say. "You weren't there, were you? She probably just said good night, politely. Why are you trying to give the girl a bad name?"

"It seems to me, you and your friend here," Pearl says, pointing at Rosie, "are no better. It's a disgrace letting young girls travel alone on a ship, speaking to strange men, asking them for favors. You think I haven't noticed?"

Tanya and Riva go into action. They get up from their bunks, daring Pearl to say another word.

Tanya, her cheeks on fire, says, "Be quiet, you old crow. Isn't it enough that one of us has been attacked for no reason and that a bitter old maid like you, with not a good word to say about anything or anyone, should spread such ugly gossip? We all heard about what happened. It was a bad incident: a sailor, who should not have been down here, tried to make advances to the first woman he could find alone. It was reported to the captain, I hear, though with people like you to spread lies, I hope no more will come of it."

Riva steps closer to Pearl. "Don't say even one more word about this, and don't you dare speak unkindly to Miriam and Rosie, who are always nice to everyone. We have had enough of your complaints." We all smile at Riva, showing our support for her words.

Silence, blissful silence, and for the last two days of the voyage, Pearl says nothing more than good morning and good night! Hopefully, she will mend her ways in the future, or her brother's hens will refuse to lay eggs if she so much as goes near them.

—

The final day, the fourteenth day of our voyage, has come at last. Rosie and I get up long before dawn and scrub ourselves in cold seawater. We wash our hair, braid it, and cover it with a kerchief. We dress in the clean skirts we have saved, to look our best for our arrival.

We climb the steps to the steerage deck for the last time, clutching our luggage. Both of us are too excited to speak. We push ourselves to the front of the railings – two girls among the throngs of other eager girls, men, women, and children, crowded together, waiting to catch our first glimpse of the Golden Land.

New York, America, 1910

13

ARRIVAL

Seagulls, the first we have seen, circle the ship. It had been foggy earlier, but as we approach New York Harbor, a wintry sun breaks through.

There, rising through the mist as if by magic, the Statue of Liberty appears. She is taller than I dreamed she would be, and her head is crowned with seven spiked rays. In her right hand, she holds a torch aloft; in her left, she clasps a book. Just as the poem says, she welcomes us all.

We have come from shtetls and cities; many of us from hostile, inhospitable, poverty-stricken countries. We have endured the harshness and indignities of the journey, as others have done before us. We have arrived at last. The journey has made me grow up. I am so full of hope, I feel as if I will burst with joy. All I can do is to gasp at the wonder of the skyline in front of us.

We are pushed against the rails by a thousand bodies. Close by, Anna and Eva stand beside their bearded young husbands. Fanny lifts Essie up to wave to the many ferryboats and ships circling the harbor.

I turn to see an old man swaying back and forth in prayer. *Does he murmur words of gratitude for our safe arrival, or does he ask for help to overcome the last and greatest hurdle we all must face?* Some call Ellis Island the Island of Tears. Tears of joy by those who are admitted to America; tears of sorrow and despair by those denied the dream.

How can I think of such a possibility, after coming all this way? Rosie and I clasp hands, marveling at the wonderful sight that greets us: a skyline decorated with immense buildings, the splendid busy harbor. As our ship draws nearer to shore, we can see the red halls on Ellis Island. Very soon, we will walk through those halls to discover our future.

"All will be well, Miriam," Rosie says, reading my thoughts.

I adjust the tag pinned to my shawl to make sure it is fixed on firmly. All passengers must wear this label, numbered and lettered, to identify who we are. Our names have to match the ship's list. If I lose my tag, I might be lost and wander forever. When Papa asks for us, probably unaware that I am here alone, the officer would look at his list, shrug, and say, "They are not here."

The gangway is lowered, and, in groups, we are hurried into waiting ferries, which bring us the short distance to

Ellis Island. I crane my neck to see the statue towering over us, closer now. Kolya said she is over three hundred feet tall.

We have arrived! Climbing onto the quay, Rosie and I hang on to each other for balance. My legs feel as if they belong to someone else. It seems strange, after all those days at sea, to tread on ground that does not move under my feet.

There is no time to get accustomed to dry land or to anything at all. In several languages, officials shout at us to hurry up, to make haste, to run. *They want us to run?* Here we are, loaded with bundles, baskets, boxes, and babies in arms. As for me, I hobble like an old woman, foolishly wearing boots that pinch my toes. I wore them to bring me luck – my best pair, the ones that Zayde made for me two years ago. He made them with room to grow, but I have definitely outgrown them. They still look like new, the leather soft and clean. My other pair is shabby, stained with salt water, and I do so want to look my best to meet Papa.

Rosie says, "Quickly, Miriam, you must change into your other boots. If the doctors see you limping . . ." We hang back. I pull my old worn pair out of the case before we hurry up the steps and into the great hall. There is no time to admire the lofty tiled roof or the pretty windows shaped like stars, set high over the balcony above the staircase.

We leave our luggage in the baggage room, downstairs. Then, they hustle us into lines separated by railings. Officials separate men and women again, before we move up the stairs to see the doctors. They wait for us with pieces of colored chalk in their hands. Each color means something different. Two women have their sleeves marked with blue chalk and are moved away. *To where? Will they be sent back, or to a hospital for quarantine, or for further inspection?* I don't know. A woman with a constant cough is pulled out of the line. Another, with a shawl concealing a hump, is also drawn aside.

The first doctor passes Rosie and me on to the next.

I whisper my thanks to her for making me change my boots. I might have been removed for limping!

The second doctor makes me take off my kerchief, so that the nurse can inspect my hair. She wears the same pair of gloves to scrutinize every head, searching for lice and diseases of the scalp. It's all I can do not to pull away in disgust. The doctor asks us if we have diseases I have never even heard of. Luckily, we are passed again.

The third doctor is the one we all fear the most – the one with the small buttonhook that turns up our eyelids, to check for trachoma.

A nurse stands by with a bowl of disinfectant. Essie cries, but she is fine. Pearl's eyes have been red and sore for the last few days. She is sent back. *How will her brother find her?* It's a miracle she did not infect us all. Still, I feel sorry for her.

Now that we have passed the medical checks, officials group us by nationality. We wait outside a door marked

REGISTRY. This is the room where an inspector will ask us questions. For the last few days, all people talked about were the questions. *What do you answer if they ask, "Do you have work to go to?"* Tanya and Riva worry that they will be accused of taking jobs away from American applicants. Fanny tells them to say they are only being considered for work, which is true.

Rosie and I have been practicing our answers, trying to predict what the questions will be. Both Papa, in his first letter home, and women who have heard from relatives in America, have offered advice.

Rosie is with the group from Italy. We will wait for each other in the great hall, after the interrogation. We hook little fingers for luck.

These next moments will decide our future. I am going to tell the truth, only the truth. I do not want to enter America with a lie.

Fanny, Essie, and I are in the same group from Germany. Interpreters are here to help translate the questions. Even the littlest children, who can barely speak, must answer. When it is Essie's turn, they ask her name, her age, and her favorite color. She is very shy. Fanny clasps the child's hand tightly. I hold my breath, remembering Yuri's silence. It does not take much to be turned down. Fanny strokes the small girl's cheek, and though Essie speaks in a whisper, it is good enough, and they are passed.

Now it is my turn. The inspector asks me, "What is your name?"

"Miriam Markov, sir."

"How old are you?"

"I am fourteen years old."

"Can you read and write?"

I nod. My mouth has gone dry. I manage, "Yes, sir."

"Read this sentence." The inspector points to some words on a board.

I read them.

"Now, write your name."

I do so, hoping this is the last question.

"Who paid for your ticket?" he asks.

"My father," I answer.

"Why are you traveling alone?"

"My little sister is unwell. When she is stronger, she and my mother will come to America." I think it is better not to mention Yuri.

"Where are you staying in America?"

I show the inspector the piece of paper with Papa's address on it.

"Do you have a job to go to?"

"No, sir."

"What kind of work can you do?"

"I can keep house for my father. I can cook, and I know how to sew."

"Are you bringing any money to America?"

"I have a little, enough for food and to help with the rent for a short while. I do not know how much it is in American money, sir."

The inspector seems satisfied and admits me to America. No more questions! I can go downstairs. Now I would like to run, but this once, I slow down and descend the stairs with my head held high, like an American lady.

Suddenly I am afraid. Thousands of people are here, lining up, with or without luggage. Voices shout, people cry. There is no sign of Papa. I look for Rosie everywhere. At last, I see my friend beside a tall man with black curly hair. He carries Rosie's luggage. A woman, his wife I think, tugs at his arm. I wave, calling Rosie's name. She turns, says something to the man, pulls away from him, and runs over to me.

"Miriam, I wanted them to wait to meet you, for you to meet Bruno, *mio fratello*, my brother, but Clara says they have to get back. I will find you, Miriam – I have your address. Thank you for everything!" We hug each other. A shrill voice, through the pandemonium of cries, shouts, and sobs, calls out, "Rosina, *pronto!*" Poor Rosie, her sister-in-law does sound strict. We wave good-bye.

I wait. *Where would Papa look for me?* I go to the baggage room and pick up my luggage. Outside the great hall, there is a ticket office, and people come and go. Ferries load and unload passengers. Friends and relatives look for each other. Some, as I am, are alone, hoping to see one longed for, familiar face. I notice Essie being lifted high in the air by her papa. *Where is mine?*

I walk up and down, looking for Papa. On the steps outside the building are men offering help and advice, just as in Hamburg. I remember Mama's warnings. *Do they think I'm so innocent?* A man wearing a blue cap, which has H.I.A.S. embroidered on it, comes up to me.

He speaks in Yiddish. "Is someone meeting you, miss? Do you have an address to go to?"

I want to shout for help, but instead I answer in English. "Yes, go away, please," I say. "My father is coming."

Then I hear his dear, remembered voice, "Miriam, Miriam, you are here." His arms embrace me, but I see only the face of a stranger!

I scream, "Let me go! I am waiting for my papa." When I dare to look up into his eyes, I see they are Papa's eyes. This time my scream is with happiness! "I did not know you, Papa. Where is your beard?" If Mama were here, she would say he looks like a crazy man.

"I shaved it off," Papa says, "so that I will look more like an American. You have grown so tall. Where has my little Miriam gone?" He hugs me again, then looks over my shoulder, searching for Yuri and Mama.

"Miriam, my child, where are the others? Was there a problem? Did the doctors keep them back?" Papa asks.

I stammer, "Hasn't Mama written to you, Papa?"

He says, "Why would she write, when we will see each other so soon?"

The man in the blue cap comes over to us and asks if we need some help. I whisper to Papa that he is a bad man. "I think he wanted me to go with him."

Papa laughs. I'd forgotten how beautiful that sound is. "Miriam, he is a good man. Every day, he comes to Ellis Island to help travelers who have no place to go. He is from the Hebrew Immigrant Aid Society."

So then I thank the man for his kindness and tell him everything is all right now.

But I must tell Papa the truth. It cannot wait. I look at him, unable to find the right words. This is the moment I have been dreading.

"They are not coming," Papa says. "I see it in your face. Is Mama sick, Yuri, the baby? Not Bubbe or Zayde? You must tell me, Miriam."

I have no choice, and there in the middle of the crowd, jostled by strangers, I describe what happened. I leave nothing out – from the time Yuri ran away to the decision Mama made in Hamburg. I give Papa her message, "'Tell Sam I will come.' There will be a letter, Papa. Mama will explain it all."

"We will talk more later," Papa says. "You must be tired. Come, a short ferry ride and we will be in our new home."

I want to cry with happiness at seeing Papa at last, but it is so sad that we are not all together yet.

"Don't cry, Miriam. You are a good brave girl, and Mama will join us later." He takes my hand. "Look about you. Welcome to America," he says.

14

A NEW WORLD

74 Clinton Street
Lower East Side
New York
America
March 3, 1910

Dear Mama,

Here I am, on my third day in New York, and there is so much to write about that I don't know where to begin. Did Papa tell you in his letter – the one from you arrived the day after I landed – that I did not recognize him without his beard?

I made a wonderful friend on the voyage. She is from Italy, and her name is Rosina, but I call her Rosie. I did not think that I would ever find another friend I like as much as Malka. We helped each other on the journey.

Steerage was crowded and not very clean. But we got enough to eat and in a proper dining room. We had one bad storm but managed to survive! Devora will be fine, Mama. The children get milk to drink and play on deck when the weather is fair enough.

When we first set eyes on the Statue of Liberty, I understood why everyone dreams of the Golden Land. The statue is more wonderful than you can ever imagine.

The apartment is nice, just as Papa described. And we do have windows. Mama, it is the law here. Every apartment has its own small fire escape. Often it is boarded up, to use as extra living, play, or storage space. Many people sleep there in summer. When you come, we can sit and drink our tea there and watch what is going on in the street below! Night and day, there is life, Mama. The shops stay open very late. You cannot imagine how many people live on the Lower East Side. I don't even know the number who live and work in our tenement building. Papa says it is called a sweatshop when one whole family, and the outsiders they hire, turn their apartment into a workplace.

People come and go day and night, working and sleeping at all hours. Their boots clatter up and down the wooden stairs. There is never a moment of silence in the Lower East Side. Whatever the hour, there is activity in the streets.

It's hard waiting until you join us, Mama. On my first evening, Mrs. Minnie Singer, the janitor, introduced herself by telling me she is not related to Singer sewing machines. I thought that was funny. Papa's sewing machine stands in the living room. Seeing it there made me feel right at home. He says his friend Boris Laski, whom he met on the boat, picked it up "cheap." Papa says all it needed was a bit of oil and kindness.

Mrs. Singer collects the rent, and scrubs and sweeps the building. She came to welcome me with her daughter, Beckie, who is a little older than I am. They brought a poppy seed cake. Wasn't that kind?

The Singers live on the ground floor and pay a reduced rent, Papa says, because she works in the building. Mrs. Singer watches everyone who comes in and goes out, and already I have heard her shout at the lodgers. "Put your cigarettes out! Do you want to start a fire?" she hollers.

Papa explained that fires often start in these wooden tenements. Mr. Singer works with Papa for J.M. Cohen and Co. They are both senior sewing-machine operators in the factory, and that's how Papa heard about the apartment. He said, when they have an hour to spare, he and Mr. Singer go the public library and play chess. When the evenings are warm enough, they even play outside in Seward Park, and Boris Laski likes to join them.

Beckie says she will take me to English class, one evening soon. It is free for everyone, Mama, and so is the library. There are lectures and discussions on all manner of things, and you can even take dance classes. I'd like to do that. There is so much to do here that I wonder anyone ever stays home! For five cents – a nickel – you can go to see moving pictures!

Beckie and I went the public baths, which are near us. For a few cents, we were given a square of soap and a clean towel. I stood in a cubicle, and water like warm rain fell down from the ceiling when I pulled a handle. All the dirty water flowed down a drain in the floor. It is so much easier than heating kettle after kettle to fill a washtub in the kitchen. Best of all, I don't have to throw the dirty water away or scrub out the tub.

We have a gas meter on the kitchen wall, and if you put a penny in, it heats the water. You do not need to worry, Mama, I will be very careful to save money and not be extravagant. I hope to find work this week.

Papa showed me the bank where he exchanged the money I had sewn into my skirt hem. Do you know this bank is the tallest building on the Lower East Side? There is a neon sign on top. On one side, the letters are in Yiddish, and on the other, in English. Papa said when the president of the bank came over to America, he started off with a pushcart!

The money I brought from Berlin, after Papa exchanged it, came to twenty American dollars. He is very pleased that it is nearly two months' rent. He gave me three dollars to buy food.

We think that we should look for a boarder to help out. It seems wasteful to have four rooms for only two people!

Today, Papa and I went for a walk after supper. I had made him potato knishes — I must have spent an hour grating the potatoes. He said it was so nice to come home after work and eat supper at his own kitchen table. He is happy not to be a boarder anymore.

He showed me Hester and Orchard streets, where you can hardly walk because of the many pushcarts jostling for room, crammed with all kinds of interesting things. Anything you might want, you can find: boots and shoes, new and secondhand; ladies' wear; lace and ribbons. There are books, rings and necklaces, clocks, pieces of furniture, gloves and hats, and bolts of cloth.

Mama, there are shops filled with so much food that my mouth waters, even after I have just eaten! To celebrate my arrival, Papa bought me a sour pickle for two cents. Big wooden barrels of sweet and sour pickles stand on the sidewalks, tempting passersby to go inside the shops.

It feels good to have a father who takes me out and explains things. Papa wants to make sure that I get used to the Golden Land, and the way of life here, before I start work. I don't remember ever spending so much time with him.

My holiday will end soon. Beckie works for a company that makes shirtwaists. She knows how anxious I am to begin earning my keep, and tomorrow, she will introduce me to one of the supervisors. She says they are always looking for girls with sewing experience.

Beckie told me about a big strike that ended a few weeks ago. Thousands of female garment workers left their machines and walked out. They refused to go back to work until hours and pay improved. Some of the men came out on strike in sympathy.

Isn't it wonderful that girls and women have such rights? Some strikers even went to prison. They didn't get all they asked for, but they won shorter hours and better wages.

I hope I get taken on at the Triangle Waist Company. Papa bought me a gift of lace. I trimmed the blouse I am going to wear for the interview with it. The new collar and cuffs look very elegant. I am lucky that you and Bubbe have taught me so well. It gives me a bit more confidence for my interview.

One day, when my English is better, I might learn to take shorthand and typing, and then I could become a secretary! Beckie thinks being a salesgirl, even in Macy's, is very tiring because you have to stand up all day. Mama, can you believe the girls are never allowed to sit down?

Also, Beckie says we can earn more in the clothing factory.

Papa put up a wooden shelf in the kitchen for our single candlestick, and we have decided to go on using an old brass pair that Boris bought secondhand for him. They look better, now that I have given them a good polish. The best moment will be when the matching one is on the Sabbath table. The one you will bring with you!

My hand aches from writing so much. I forgot to mention there is an important newspaper here that Papa and Mr. Singer take in turns to read. It is called the Jewish Daily Forward. *I will send you a copy. It is written in Yiddish. Readers write letters to the editor for the column "The Bintel Brief," for all kinds of advice, such as who to marry or troubles with in-laws. Some letters are funny; some are sad. But there are political ideas and news too.*

I send a kiss to my little Devora.

Love from your daughter,

Miriam

I have not told Mama everything. I don't want her to worry. Yes, we have windows – small ones, but only one of them lets in daylight. The second one looks into an airshaft, which smells bad from the garbage people throw down there.

I would never tell Mama Mrs. Singer's first question to me. It would grieve her so much to hear it. She asked, "Where are your mama, the little daughter, and the boy?"

The look that passed over Papa's face almost made me cry.

"They will come later," he said. "The baby is delicate." Then Mrs. Singer apologized for barging in. I do like her and her daughter, Beckie.

On Sunday, Papa went to work to make up for the time he has taken off. I have just come back from a short walk in Seward Park. Some spring shoots are already coming out. What a great country this is! To think that the city made a park, right here, on the Lower East Side. It means so much to everyone who lives in our crowded tenement buildings. The park is always full of people, who enjoy walking among trees and flowers. Children play on the grass, not just in the streets. I walk on my own, no Bubbe or Mama to tell me not to wander out alone. It is a strange feeling.

I put on the kettle for a glass of tea, feeling just a little lonely. I started the soup for tonight's supper earlier. I got a nice beef bone from the butcher, threw a chopped onion into the pan, along with some sliced carrots and potatoes, and left it all to simmer. It smells good.

I hear steps on the stairs. They hesitate. It is too early for Papa to be home. Someone taps on the door. I open it cautiously, wondering who it could be.

"Rosie! Oh, what a wonderful surprise! Come in, I never expected to see you so soon." We hug each other as though we have been parted for weeks, instead of days.

15

ROSIE

"I can't believe it's really you, Rosie. Sit down. Make yourself comfortable."

Rosie says, "I can't tell you how much I've missed you these last few days, Miriam."

"Me, too. I was just making tea, wishing I had a friend to talk to. Now we can catch up. I hope you have time to stay and meet Papa. Are you hungry? There is some cake left. Our janitor, Mrs. Singer, baked it. It is a few days old, but it still tastes good."

I bring two glasses of tea to the table, a few slices of lemon on a saucer, a couple of sugar lumps, and the remaining slices of cake.

"Dunk the cake in your tea, if you want. Do you remember how we had to dip Bubbe's black bread in salt water to soften?" Rosie starts to laugh, but suddenly, her laughter turns to tears. *She can't be crying over that, can she?* I wait, feeling helpless. I don't know how to comfort her.

Rosie mops her cheeks. "I'm so relieved to see you, Miriam. There is no one else I can turn to."

"Isn't that what friends are for? Tell me what's wrong, Rosie. Did something happen at home?"

She nods, and her words come spilling out. "Maybe I was expecting too much. I've felt so unwelcome, Miriam. Clara, my brother's wife, told me to go. Bruno brought me. He is waiting outside, to make sure I'm all right. I had to bring my things. May I tell him that I can stay here for a few days, just till I have found work? I told him and Clara that I have friends in New York."

"Of course you can. It is perfectly true, you do have friends: Papa and I are your friends. I've told him so much about you, Rosie. I am sorry you are upset, but I'd love you to stay with us. Papa and I have been saying we should take in a boarder. It will be a while before Mama and the children are here. Let's go and tell your brother."

We run downstairs. Her brother waits, suitcase in hand, pacing up and down the sidewalk. Rosie speaks to him in Italian. I can't understand more than a word or two, other than my name.

Bruno walks over to me and shakes my hand. "Thank you for being such a good friend to my sister," he says. He embraces Rosie and passes her suitcase to her. "I will keep in touch, little one. I am sorry things turned out badly." He kisses Rosie on both cheeks and strides away.

We go back upstairs. I make fresh tea. I know that I am being a bit extravagant. But this once, even Mama would agree that it is the right thing to do on such a special occasion.

"Rosie, your brother seems so nice. How did all this happen?" I ask.

She says, "Nothing went right from the very start. Don't you remember how Clara wouldn't even wait for me to introduce you to her at Ellis Island? I don't think she ever wanted me to come. She has never, once, tried to make me feel welcome. In fact, just the opposite. Her first words to me when we got home were 'I've arranged for you to start at the commercial laundry down the street. The manager will see you tonight, after supper. They stay open late, and if you suit him, you can begin tomorrow. Starting pay is six dollars for a six-day week, twelve-to-fourteen-hour shifts. If you work night shifts, you earn fifty cents more. You'll give me five dollars a week for your keep. The rest is your own. What do you say?' I was speechless!

"Clara seemed very pleased with herself. Her grand-mother, who lives with them, nodded away, smiling. I was shocked that Clara had not even asked me what kind of work I wanted to do. I hadn't even had a chance to unpack!

"Bruno said, 'Clara, what can you be thinking? No sister of mine is going to work there. It's dangerous. Accidents happen all the time. Heavy machinery, having to carry loads she'd barely manage to lift, working day and night in a damp basement, Rosie would end up like Papa, her lungs ruined. I forbid it. Look at her – she's not strong enough for that kind of work. We'll find her something easier, maybe working in one of the bakeries as a salesgirl.'

"I was glad Bruno stood up for me, but that was the only time. He's weak, where Clara is concerned. She does not like to be contradicted. I watched her lips clamp shut, her eyes grow hard. From then on, it was war between us.

"Bruno had to leave for his night shift. He's a construction worker, who helped build the Manhattan Bridge. Now he works underground, building a subway. That is dangerous work. He needs to concentrate, not worry over Clara and me!

"Nothing I could say or do was right from that moment on. The old lady was worse than Clara. She complained about me from morning to night. Yesterday I made pasta. I've been rolling out pasta and making tomato sauce since I was a little girl. Papa taught me. When Bruno tasted the sauce, he kissed his fingers, praised my cooking, and said it was as good as eating back home with our parents.

"Marco, one of his construction-worker friends who had been invited for supper, joined in the praise. 'That is the best spaghetti I've tasted since I left Naples. Your little sister will be in great demand, Bruno,' he said. He winked at me, flirting a bit, Miriam. It meant nothing. I thanked him, that's all. I could tell Clara was furious. She turned bright red and glared at Bruno.

"'How is it you never praise my cooking, Bruno? Maybe your sister should take over.' You can imagine how I felt, being the cause of a family quarrel. I excused myself to go and bring in the coffee. Then I went out again to wash the dishes. I overheard Clara's raised voice and my name. It's hard feeling unwanted. I almost wished I'd stayed in Hamburg. I was so upset that I dropped a plate.

"Clara and her grandmother came in, calling me careless and clumsy. Of course, I apologized and offered to buy a new plate. They waved their hands about and carried on, saying it was irreplaceable, part of a set. Honestly, I don't think they were that upset about the plate. It just gave them an excuse to make me feel bad.

"Clara said, 'Decent Italian girls don't make eyes at strange men.'

"Do you know who Clara reminds me of, Miriam? Pearl! Bruno came in to see what the shouting was about.

"Clara said, 'You had better find your sister another place to live. She does not fit in here. I will not have her in my house a moment longer than necessary.'

"I said, 'That suits me fine. I don't need to stay where I'm not wanted. I'll pack my things. I have a place to go – friends I can stay with.' So here I am."

A tear trickles down Rosie's cheek, and this time, I join

in out of sympathy. I've never heard of anything so sad. To be thrown out after coming all this way! Clara does sound like Pearl. Her brother never stood up to her either! Neither of us notice that Papa has come in.

"What is wrong? Has something happened to Mama?" he says.

"No, Papa. Don't look so worried. We were just talking. This is Rosie," I say. I dry my eyes.

Papa shakes hands with her. "I feel I know you already, Rosie," he says. "Welcome. You are the great friend from the ship, isn't that right? So maybe you can tell me what kind of 'talking' has made you both cry?"

Rosie explains. Papa listens carefully. "For every problem," he says, "there is a solution. That is what my father-in-law, Miriam's Zayde, always says. In this instance, I see no problem, only the solution.

"If your mama were here, Miriam, she would say to Rosie, 'Sit down, eat, you are welcome to stay for as long as you like.' So this is what I say too. Please, make yourself at home, Rosie."

I set three places and serve the soup that has been ready for an hour! It feels right to have Rosie here. I'm happy because we have found a perfect boarder, who just happens to be my best friend too!

Papa says, "This soup is so good, I swear it could have been made by Bubbe. Now let's speak about sleeping arrangements. Mine is the biggest room, Miriam, so you and Rosie will take it, and I will be fine in the smaller one. No buts, only promise me that you will not talk all night. Do we have a deal?"

"It is a perfect solution, thank you, Papa. *Perfetto*, isn't it, Rosie?" I say.

"Thank you very much, Mr. Markov, and please, sir, I can pay for my board. My brother, Bruno, gave me five dollars. Also I have a little saved."

Papa says, "No, no, it can wait. We shall discuss payment after you find work. For now, keep your money. Girls, this is enough excitement for one evening. I am going to read my newspaper!"

We have just finished putting Rosie's things away, when Beckie knocks on the door. She has called to remind me to be ready at seven o'clock in the morning. As if I could forget! We'll walk together to the Triangle Waist Company. Work does not start until 8:15 a.m., but there's the interview to get through first. I introduce my friends to each other.

Beckie makes a wonderful suggestion: "Anna Gullo, the foreman who does the hiring, asked me if I know of any other girls looking for work. Do you have a job yet, Rosie?"

Rosie says, "Not yet. I thought of trying to find work in a bakery."

Beckie says, "Mr. Bernstein, the factory manager, says they are swamped with orders for the new season. Why don't you come with us? Maybe you'll both get taken on. We get forty-five minutes for lunch. I bring a nickel and buy something from a vendor or go to a café near the factory. In a couple of weeks, it will be warmer. Then I'll bring a sandwich and eat in the park.

"Before the strike," Beckie says, "we had to work twelve-hour shifts in the busy season. We had barely half an hour for lunch. We often worked seven days a week. Now, there's time to get a bit of fresh air on our break."

Rosie smiles and smiles. Everything is working out well. I'm happy my friends have met and seem to like each other.

Papa says, "You see, everything is turning out for the best. You are saving ten cents by walking to work, so take two nickels for your lunch from the housekeeping jar. If you don't get hired tomorrow, then keep them for the next time. Please don't forget your papa's bottle of tea, Miriam." Papa looks as proud as if he'd personally arranged the interview for us!

16

THE TRIANGLE
WAIST COMPANY

It is exciting to be walking with Rosie and Beckie to my first job interview. Beckie is a sleeve setter on the eighth floor of the Triangle Waist Company. She's been there a year, making shirtwaists, since she was almost fourteen.

"I started off by sewing buttons on shirtwaists, at seven dollars a week," Beckie says. "Now I make eleven!"

"I am not sure what you call a shirtwaist," I say to her.

"It's just a fancy name for a blouse with a high collar and full sleeves, which you wear tucked into a skirt. All over America, rich and poor girls and women wear shirtwaists. They can be plain or fancy, pleated or embroidered."

Beckie never seems to stop talking or giving us advice. Already she has become like an old friend and taken us under her wing. She's determined to turn us into American girls, in the shortest time possible.

Rosie asks her, "How long have you lived in New York, Beckie? You know so much."

"My family came here from Russia, from Kishinev, when I was eight. That was in 1903, a year of terrible pogroms. We were lucky to escape. My father does not like to speak of it. He lost many relatives."

I squeeze her arm in sympathy. I remember Papa, Zayde, and Kolya talking about that dreadful time. Thank goodness the pogroms cannot follow us here.

I try sounding out the names of the streets to help me memorize them. After only a week here, there are still many new things to learn.

Seward Park is quiet this early in the day, but the streets bustle with life. Women shout last-minute instructions as they send off their husbands and children to work or school. Peddlers push their carts to the market on Hester and Orchard streets, eager to get hold of early customers. That's the pig market, which in Yiddish is called the *chazir-mark*. It seems odd to call it that, when you can buy or sell almost anything there, except pork.

Many people go to the market when they first arrive in America, hoping to get hired for casual work. I wouldn't like to be one of them. Imagine having to stand, in front of all those strangers, like a piece of merchandise waiting to be picked over.

"Hey, girl, we need some finishers," people hiring call out to the women and girls. Rosie and I are lucky to have Beckie to introduce us at the factory. I'm feeling nervous. This is the first time I've been interviewed for a job. All I've ever done is to help Mama and Bubbe. *What will they want to know?* Rosie must be wondering the same thing.

She says, "It can't be any worse than the questions they asked us in Hamburg or on Ellis Island."

It's still early. Storekeepers open their shutters, sweep their front steps, and display their wares temptingly on the sidewalk. Boys shine windows or shoes. They run errands or sell newspapers, before going to school. Yuri might have been one of them, if he hadn't been so stubborn! We walk along Rivington Street, then East Houston, past many stores and cafés.

There are so many sights for me to write home about. No, not home. Home is where I live now. But to the rest of the family, who waits for news from me before they leave Berlin to join us.

Beckie points to a ten-storey skyscraper. "We're almost there. That's the Asch Building. The Triangle Waist Company is on the eighth, ninth, and tenth floors."

"Yes, I can see the sign, Beckie. Look, Rosie, up there!"

"The building takes over the whole corner of Washington Place and Greene Street. See how it juts out, like the prow of a ship?" Beckie says.

Mama will be so surprised when I write her that I am working in a skyscraper – that is, if I am hired! I ask Beckie, "Who owns the factory?"

"Mr. Max Blanck and Mr. Isaac Harris own it. Mr. Harris roams the floors, making sure the work is done exactly the way he wants it. He designs many of the shirtwaists. In the busy season, we turn out twelve thousand shirtwaists or more in a week. Mr. Harris doesn't talk to any of us machinists – I doubt he even knows our names. No girl would ever dare to speak to him first. We're expected to keep our eyes on our work."

"What exactly do the machinists sew, Beckie? Does each girl make a whole shirtwaist?" Rosie asks.

"Each machinist is responsible for a different part of the shirtwaist: the collar, cuffs, sleeves, bodices, buttons, and buttonholes. Then the pieces are taken up to the ninth floor by the floor girls, to be assembled. The tenth, the top floor, is the showroom. The pressing, packing, final inspection, and shipping are done there."

"Tell us more about the bosses," Rosie says.

"Mr. Blanck meets the customers on the top floor. He also walks round the other floors, making sure the exit doors are locked. He's afraid we might smuggle a bit of lace home. Once a girl hid a shirtwaist under her hair – can you imagine? Of course she was found out, fired, and black-listed! We all have our pocketbooks searched before we go home. There's a night watchman on each floor."

Rosie and I look at each other. "That sounds awful, Beckie. I am not a thief – none of us are! Doesn't he trust his workers?" I say.

"During the strike, I heard Mr. Blanck tried to pretend he was on the side of the workers. That's a joke. I heard he invited the ones from the eighth and ninth floors who crossed the picket line to come to work, to listen to a phonograph at lunchtime. He set it up in a small space on the ninth floor, and there was dancing! He'd have done any-thing to get us to come back."

"Were you glad to go back?" Rosie asks.

"I wish we'd held out for more than we got. But how long can a girl manage without a paycheck?" Beckie says.

"I've never earned a paycheck, but I can imagine," I say, remembering how anxiously Mama used to count out the money for rent.

"You'd never think, to see them now, that Mr. Blanck and Mr. Harris came off the boat, just like we did. They're from Russia and started off working in a tenement sweatshop. Look at them now, with their swanky homes and servants. Max Blanck comes to work in a chauffeured limousine. I've even seen him wear a diamond in his lapel. They own the biggest shirtwaist factory in New York. People call them the Shirtwaist Kings.

"They hire their relatives for the top jobs. That's natural, I guess. Mr. Samuel Bernstein, who's in charge of the eighth and ninth floors, is Mr. Blanck's brother-in-law. Mr. Harris's sister, Eva, works here, and Mrs. Harris's cousin, Mary, does typing and sometimes switchboard duty."

"I hope there are some other Italian girls here," Rosie says.

"You'll be surprised how many Italian girls work here, Rosie. We all get along so well, laughing and joking when the bosses aren't looking. Since the end of the strike, wages are better, and we work shorter hours. Mind you, the bosses still get up to their old tricks."

"What do you mean, 'tricks'?" I ask.

"Sometimes they stop the clock for a few minutes to get a bit more work out of us before closing time. Or they move the clock ahead, to squeeze a few minutes from our lunch break. One of these days, I'll get myself a watch, so I can prove it. At least now we don't have to pay for our own needles. Don't be surprised, though, if the supervisor follows you into the washroom. She does that, to make sure you're not wasting time. If we get sick, we don't get paid. Not that much changed after the strike."

I'm beginning to feel more and more nervous. Even Rosie's looking worried.

"Beckie, I am not so good at sewing," Rosie says, "not like you and Miriam. What should I tell the lady when she asks me what I can do?"

"You have hemmed a dress, mended a shawl, or sewn on a button, haven't you?" Beckie asks her. Rosie nods a bit uncertainly. "So tell Anna Gullo, our foreman, that you do plain sewing. The machines do most of the work because they are all connected to one electric motor. All you have to do is to press the floor pedal and feed the cloth through the machine. It's easy when you get used to it. I prefer it here to working in a department store. I know it means sitting for a long time, and you have to concentrate, but it's a lot better than not being allowed to sit at all."

Beckie gestures as she speaks, so that Rosie can follow what she is saying. We both practice our English as much as we can. And Papa says we should all speak only English at supper. I wonder how long he'll keep that up!

"You'll be fine," Beckie says. "Let's hope neither one of you has to work the buttonhole machine, on the ninth floor. It's forever breaking down, and then the shirtwaists pile up and the foreman goes wild!"

"Another park," I say.

"That's Washington Square Park over there, with a white arch over the north entrance. We've no time to go in now, but one Sunday, or Saturday after work, we will. It's a lovely place at any time of year. People are always out strolling, and children can play away from the streets. We're almost there now," Beckie says.

"Is this where we go in?" I ask.

"No, this is the main entrance for the Triangle Waist Company, on the Washington Place side. It's reserved for customers and the bosses, who use the two smaller passenger elevators to go up to the tenth floor. Our entrance is farther down, round the corner, here on Greene Street. We use one of two freight elevators. There's room for up to fifteen workers at a time. You'll always see a line waiting to go up. No one wants to be docked pay for being late," Beckie explains.

As we arrive, some workers are already waiting. When we get on the elevator, Beckie introduces us to Joseph Zito, one of the two operators. There's barely time to exchange remarks about the weather before we reach the eighth floor. I've never been on an elevator before, but I don't say anything. I don't want to be called a greenhorn. We step out and Beckie turns right, past a door which she says opens into the staircase leading both to the top floor and down to Greene Street. She points to a clock, which is set high in a wooden partition. Beside it is the single door through which the workers enter onto the work floor, or shop, as it is sometimes called.

"We are in plenty of time. This is where Mr. Wexler, the night watchman, stands. He can see right across the floor.

He rings the starting and quitting bells. At night, he checks our pocketbooks. On the ninth floor, the other night watchman does the same.

"We should go in now and see Miss Gullo."

One by one, we pass through the narrow door and enter the shop. It feels bright and airy. Light streams in through the floor-to-ceiling windows. Beckie takes us into the dressing room, which has lockers and a full-length mirror. We hang up our things and smooth our hair. I don't want to look windswept when I meet Miss Gullo.

Beckie says, "If either of you gets sent to work on the ninth floor, we'll meet downstairs, outside the Greene Street elevators, at lunchtime."

There are rows of long tables, at which cutters and their assistants are getting ready for the day. The table legs are boarded up from the floor to a few inches below the tabletops. They form a bin, into which scraps of leftover material are pushed out of the way by the cutters. Beckie says a rag dealer empties the bins when they are full.

Papa has told me that cutters are top men in the trade who get the highest wages because they are the most skilled. The cutters arrange the patterns, so that the least possible material is wasted as they cut into layers of fabric. Flimsy paper patterns dangle from wires strung over the tables, swaying like cutout dolls.

Beckie said there are forty cutters on this floor. I can

see them at five tables on one side of the shop, under the windows overlooking Greene Street, and two more on the Washington Place side. Tables with sewing machines fill the remainder of the room. How I hope that Rosie and I will soon join Beckie at one of them!

There is so much to look at. Lining the walls at intervals are red fire buckets filled with water. A few stand on shelves above some of the cutting tables. There are big signs saying NO SMOKING in Italian, English, and Yiddish. But I notice one of the cutters holding up his jacket to hide his cigarette!

We follow Beckie to a small desk that stands between two cutting tables and the dressing room. Two women greet us with a smile. One is seated.

"Good morning, girls. I am Anna Gullo, foreman for the ninth floor," says the one standing, "and this is Dinah Lipschitz, our eighth-floor bookkeeper. She keeps account of everything that is produced on this floor."

Miss Lipschitz writes down our names, and Miss Gullo asks Rosie what kind of sewing experience she has had.

"I can do plain sewing, miss," Rosie says, confidently repeating Beckie's instruction. She smiles. That smile will get her anything.

Miss Gullo tells her she'll start her on the ninth floor as a hemmer.

When it's my turn, I tell Miss Gullo that my father is a tailor and that I've been doing all kinds of sewing since I was a little girl. She asks me if I made my blouse and looks closely at the stitching. I'm thrilled when she says she'll try me out as a cuff setter, at Beckie's table. This means I'll be adding cuffs to shirtwaist sleeves.

We are both hired!

Miss Gullo says, "Mr. Bernstein will inform Miss Lipschitz at the end of the day what your wages will be. The working week is fifty-two hours, from 8:15 a.m. to 6:00 p.m. Monday to Friday, with a lunch break of forty-five minutes. The short day is on Saturday, from 9:00 a.m. to 4:45 p.m. Saturday is payday. There may also be work on Sundays. Rosina, I'll take you up to the ninth floor now. Go and collect your things from the dressing room. Beckie, please show Miriam to your table. She will sit between Annie and Nettie."

Rosie hurries back to the dressing room. She manages a quick wave to us before following Miss Gullo.

It's wonderful and a bit frightening to think that, in just a few minutes, I have become a working girl in the biggest and most modern shirtwaist factory in New York. Maybe in the whole world!

17

MIRACLE ON THE
EIGHTH FLOOR

A supervisor shows me what to do. After she leaves, I introduce myself to the girls sitting on either side of me. They offer to help, if something goes wrong. I'm really nervous now. *Suppose I break the needle?* A girl, her hair covered by a kerchief, runs in. She takes her place, next to Beckie and directly across from me.

She gasps, breathless. "I thought I'd be late, Beckie. My mother isn't feeling well, and I had to deliver some laundry for her. I only just made it in time." The girl's voice sounds familiar. *But where have I heard it before?* She stares at me, and shivers run up and down my back.

"You've gone as white as a sheet, Miriam. Don't be afraid; you'll be fine," Beckie says.

Can it be true? Is it possible that Malka, the first friend I ever had, is sitting opposite me? I wonder if she remembers how we played in the shtetl. How we ran, hand in hand, away from the Cossacks. At school in Kiev, we sat next to each other. We were inseparable. Then one day she was gone, and no one knew where. If they did, they were afraid to tell me. *How can she be here?* We both begin speaking at exactly the same time.

"Malka Pinski, I can't believe it, is it you?" I whisper, almost afraid to ask.

Malka says, "Miriam! Miriam Markowitz, are you a ghost? Beckie, pinch me, I'm dreaming. Ouch, no, I'm not." We both stand up and push back our chairs, so we can run to each other.

At that moment, the bell goes. The power is switched on, and the machines begin to clack and clatter. Annie pulls me down. I sit, tense, terrified that I can't do this. The machine is so much faster than the old treadle I'm used to. I concentrate on feeding the cloth smoothly under the needle. Gradually, I find a rhythm. My thoughts race faster than any machine. The noise around me is constant, loud, but I don't mind. I like helping to make clothes for women all over the country to wear. Only, now, all my thoughts are with Malka. I am overwhelmed by the need to speak. I have so many things to ask her: *Did she know she was going to America? Does she still make dresses for her doll?* Of course not, we are the same age – fourteen! We put away our dolls a long time ago. I don't dare to look up from my work yet. The floor girl throws another pile of cuffs into the wicker basket at my feet.

At last, I feel confident enough to take my eyes off the machine for a second to smile at Malka. I want to ask her how she got here and how long ago she came to America.

Before I can get the words out, she mutters, "Bernstein's coming." Just in time, I smooth the cloth before it puckers. The manager stands and watches me work for a moment or two, before moving on. It's hard to speak, but every now and then, we look up and smile at each other.

At last, the longest morning of my life comes to an end. The bell rings for the lunch break. Gratefully, I stand up and stretch. My wrists ache, my back is stiff, and there's a ringing in my ears from the hum of the machines. It doesn't matter. All that matters is that Malka and I have found each other again.

In the dressing room, we fall into each other's arms, laughing and crying with happiness. Girls mill round us, not taking any notice. Lockers open and close. Everyone is anxious to make the most of the only break of the day.

Beckie tells us not to waste precious time. We hurry into the elevator. Rosie is there before us, with some girls from the ninth floor, talking to Gaspar Mortillalo, the second elevator operator.

"Did it go well, Rosie?" I ask her.

"I think so. You were right about the buttonhole machine, Beckie. I felt sorry for the boy in charge of it. You look as if something wonderful has happened, Miriam. Tell me!"

The moment the elevator stops and we scramble out, Malka and I explain the miracle of finding each other.

Beckie says, "Are we going to live on air? I am starving. Come on, Mrs. Lena Goldman's café is just a short way up Greene Street. Several of the girls go there for lunch."

Malka says, "I brought a sandwich, but I'll get a glass of tea."

We don't stop talking, except to tell Mrs. Goldman that the three of us will have her lunch special of tea and coffee cake for a nickel. We settle into a booth for four. There are menu items chalked up on a board over the till, and red checked curtains at the window. I have never eaten in a café before. But I don't feel like a greenhorn, I'm too happy.

"Miriam, tell me about the family," Malka says. "Are you all in New York now?"

"Only Papa and me, the others will come later. My little sister, Devora, is only two, and not strong enough for the voyage yet. I came on ahead."

"A new sister, how lovely!" Malka says. "You are brave to come here alone, Miriam. You were always braver than me." I blush at the compliment.

"Tell me about your family," I say.

"Mother does fine laundry for wealthy customers. Esther,

my sister, is married. She has a baby boy, Abbie, short for Abraham. Do you remember my brother, Reuven? He is studying at night classes to become a waiter. During the day, he delivers for Katz's Delicatessen, at Ludlow and East Houston."

"We should all go there after work, one day, don't you think, girls?" Beckie says.

Rosie and I nod – our mouths are too full of cake to speak.

"Miriam, I want to hear about that rascal Yuri," Malka says.

"He is as stubborn as ever, I'm afraid. When we have more time, I'll tell you all about him. For now, it's enough for you to know that he ran away the night before we left for America! I want to hear how long you've been in New York and why you didn't tell me you were going away!" I say.

"Miriam, I wanted to tell you, but Papa made me promise not to say a word. We got out of Russia and crossed the border into Poland, hidden under potato sacks. It was many days before we arrived in Bremen. After a long wait, when we were inspected from head to toe, we were finally allowed to board the ship. It was a horrible journey. I'll never set foot on another ship as long as I live!

"Beckie and I started work almost at the same time, last year. Up till then, I helped Mama with the laundry and did mending. Mr. Blanck's wife, Bertha, sends Mama her lingerie! I wonder what she'd say if she knew one of the machinists in her husband's factory knows the color of her petticoats!" We can't stop laughing.

Beckie says, "We've been sitting next to each other for a year, Malka. I thought I knew all about you. I can't get over you two meeting like this."

Malka says, "It still seems like a dream. Tell me how long you've been in New York, Miriam."

"I arrived only a week ago. It seems longer – so much has happened. Papa has been here for two years. We lived in Berlin after we left Kiev. Our journey here wasn't too bad. Rosie and I met in Hamburg and became friends. Now she boards with us. It is a small world – we even live in the same house as Beckie on Clinton Street! Papa said yesterday that every time he goes to play chess or walks to the *chazir-mark*, he meets someone he knows from Kiev!"

Rosie says, "It is, how you say? *Destino*, fate. It is meant to be that we four should be together!"

Beckie looks up at the clock above the till. "If we don't hurry back, it will be 'fate' to be docked pay for being late!"

We laugh some more, eat the last crumbs of the delicious cake, pay, and make our way back to work.

"It's not fair, Miriam, you are still taller than me," Malka says.

"And you are as skinny as ever! Do you remember how we used to pester Papa to measure us, to see who was the tallest? You have hardly mentioned your father, Malka. How is he?"

"Papa died of tuberculosis two years ago, Miriam. Mama thinks he must have caught it on the ship. The men's quarters were very crowded and dirty, he told us."

"I am so sorry, Malka." I wish, now, that I had not asked.

We get back to work just before the bell goes. The afternoon seems endless. Floor girls run back and forth. Mr. Bernstein walks round the tables making sure the work is going smoothly, and I long to get up and stretch. My back is not used to being hunched over a sewing machine all day. There is no Mama or Bubbe to say, "Time for a glass of tea."

Malka says, "Turn your head for a second, Miriam. Mr. Blanck is checking the Washington Place door, again." I glance behind me but don't manage to get a good look at the boss.

A supervisor appears. She says, "Keep your eyes on your work."

Finally, the quitting bell rings. I feel as if I've been sitting crouched over a table for a week! We hurry to put on our coats. There is already a lineup to get through the partition. I hate the idea of having my pocketbook searched.

"You'll get used to it, Miriam," Beckie says. I suppose so. I manage to smile and say good night to Mr. Wexler. What a relief to get down to Greene Street. I'm glad of the walk, after a long day of sitting down. Malka lives on Rivington Street, so we can walk part of the way home with her. We arrange to meet again, next morning. I'm too excited, now, to feel tired and can't wait to go home and tell Papa every-thing that has happened today.

I decide to bring Malka my outgrown boots that Zayde made for me. They still look good as new. She is so tiny, they'll fit her beautifully. Her boots look like mine did at the end of the voyage. And although I polished the salt stains away, I badly need some new ones. Mama used to give my outgrown clothes to Malka's mother for her, when we were small.

Rosie and I cook supper together, and it is almost ready when Papa comes home from work.

"Well," he says, "how did you make out? Have they hired both of you?"

"Yes, Papa, and we are each to be paid nine dollars a week!" He congratulates us and says how proud he is of us. Then I tell him about Malka. He is pleased that the Pinskis are safe in America.

"I grieve for Mrs. Pinski and the children. It is so sad to lose a father. Emanuel was a fine man," Papa says. "How tragic to come such a long way and then to die!" He sighs.

"So, are you going to tell me about the factory and what work you are doing?" Papa says.

"I'm a cuff setter on the eighth floor, Papa. It is a big square space, with high ceilings and huge windows. You never told me that the sewing machine can make thousands of stitches a minute. At first, I was scared I'd do something wrong. By the afternoon, I got used to it. What I really don't like is having my pocketbook searched, as though they suspect me of being a thief. I don't think I'll ever get used to that. Or the time it takes to get out of the building at the end of the day. The door to leave the shop floor is too narrow to allow more than one of us to pass through. But take no notice of my complaints, Papa. I know we are lucky to work at the 'Triangle.' I do like it, and it is fun working with so many girls together."

"Miriam, searching employees is the practice everywhere. It prevents dishonest workers – and there are always some – from stealing from the company. Rosie, are you on the same floor as Miriam?"

"No, Mr. Markov, I work on the ninth floor, hemming. The sewing tables and chairs are so close together on my floor, we almost have to take turns to get up and sit down. There are two hundred and forty machines. All the tables are in rows, from one end of the room to the other. I have some Italian girls at my table, and two of them are from Cherry Street, where my brother lives."

"You are lucky girls," Papa says. "The Asch Building is a new skyscraper, built of steel and concrete. I have often walked by it. A fine factory, I think. Not everything can be perfect, but it sounds as if you will do very well."

On Saturday, we all receive our paychecks. Papa suggests that Rosie pays three dollars and fifty cents a week for her board.

"Thank you so much, Mr. Markov," Rosie says. "I will be able to send money home to my parents and brothers and still have some over for myself." She starts to make her wonderful tomato sauce for supper.

Papa says, "You may keep two dollars for yourself too, Miriam. That is fair. Some you use for housekeeping, some you save for tickets for the family to join us, and the rest is for you."

"Thank you, Papa." I can't believe it. I have never had money of my own before. I can save up for a new shirtwaist or replace my boots. I can take classes in typing; I can go to the movies. Anything is possible in America!

New York, America, 1911

18

SATURDAY, MARCH 25

A whole year has gone by. Arm in arm, Rosie and I set off for work, each of us lost in our own thoughts. My dream will soon come true. Mama has written that Devora is strong enough to travel. They hope to join us in June. After all this time in America without them, I have started to mark off the days until they arrive.

Bubbe and Zayde have decided to stay behind. Mama wrote us that they feel too old to cross the ocean, to start over again in a new country. I can't imagine our family without them. Papa comforts me. He thinks they might change their minds. He believes all the "nonsense" of Yuri's rejection will be forgotten by the authorities in a year or two. I hope he is right.

Rosie is wearing a beautiful spring hat today, trimmed with a small posy of artificial daisies and violets. I have on my new, cream-colored shirtwaist. For my fifteenth birthday, Papa gave me a lovely, lightweight length of fabric and helped me make it up in the latest style. The material is so delicate, I did not trust myself to cut it. I made it with full sleeves, edging the cuffs and collar and even the buttonholes with scallops of lace.

Beckie has to stay home today. Two days ago, she pierced her finger on a needle. The wound became infected. Yesterday she came in to work, so as not to miss getting paid. Finally, her mother put her foot down and made her stay home. It is a shame because Saturday is the best day of the week. Not only is it payday, but it is a short workday. We, the Four Fates as Beckie calls us, always have a treat planned.

Sometimes we stroll in Washington Square Park, or walk along Grand Street and look at the shops. Maybe we stop for an ice-cream soda, or buy a ribbon. Best of all is when we promenade the mile across the Brooklyn Bridge, which spans the East River. We can cross in thirty minutes, if we don't stop too often. It's a wonderful way to see New York – to watch people from different parts of the city, rich and poor, strolling along together.

Malka waits for us at the corner of Rivington Street, as she does every morning. For some reason, today when I see her waiting, I breathe a sigh of relief. I think Mama's letter must have reminded me of that morning in Kiev, when Malka and her family just vanished overnight. Malka is wearing Zayde's boots again today. I can't believe that they still fit her.

We've arranged to go to Katz's Delicatessen for a soda after work. Malka's brother, Reuven, waits on tables there now. He has eyes only for Beckie and will be disappointed that she's not there. I smile at Rosie, and she smiles back, but I can tell she's miles away.

A few weeks ago, her brother, Bruno, picked her up to come to his house for supper. He and Clara have a baby boy. It is hard to imagine Rosie as an aunt! She says that she and Clara have declared a truce, though they will never be friends. At least they are speaking! Bruno's friend Marco was there for supper, too, and walked Rosie home. Since then, they have been out walking twice!

Rosie sighs happily. "I can smell spring in the air. Isn't it a perfect day?"

She must be in love because not a whisper of a breeze gets between our tenement buildings. And you have to crane your neck to catch a glimpse of a clear sky. I know what she means though – I feel spring too.

Malka says, "One day, I'm going to live in a house with big windows. I'll sleep in a room where the sun wakes me up in the morning, and I can smell grass and trees. I'll open the window wide and look up and see the sky, as blue as the ocean.

"I have a great idea," she continues. "Why don't we go to Coney Island, one Sunday, and walk along the boardwalk and by the beach? There's a trolley that goes all the way there." A gust of wind makes us shiver in our spring finery. Rosie clutches her hat. "Maybe we'd better wait a couple of weeks, till mid-April, when it's warmer," Malka says.

We hurry into work. Rosie is a floor runner now and says she enjoys it. She really does run from one floor to the other, bringing new pieces to the machinists and collecting their finished ones.

I think she knows everyone's name in the factory and is often the first one to hear any gossip. She swears us to secrecy before she'll repeat a single word! We were both given a raise two weeks ago to mark the end of our first year at the Triangle Waist Company. A whole dollar a week each!

There's no time left for talking or daydreaming. As usual, we take our seats in front of our machines moments before the starting bell rings. Malka works at a different table now.

The pace is frantic all day, typical of a Saturday at the height of the spring season. There are not enough hours left for us to fill yet another back order before Monday. New orders pour in as fast as the shirtwaists pile up at the button machine. Rosie says the machine broke down twice this morning! I doubt that we got our full lunch break today. I'm sure they fixed the clock to get us back to work earlier.

Everyone, especially on a Saturday, tries to get away the second the quitting bell sounds. Sometimes, Rosie manages a quick exit into the dressing room before the other girls. She is so particular about fixing her hair and her hat! The floor girls move between the eighth, ninth, and tenth floors all day, so they are not stuck at the machines, like we are, until the bell rings.

Malka now works on lace runners. Her table is by the windows, which overlook Greene Street, close beside one of the cutting tables. This year, I'm making collars, but Beckie still sets sleeves. She is one of the best workers on the floor.

The afternoon is worse than this morning – one of the foremen complains he has more bodices than sleeves. "Where are my missing sleeves?" he yells. "And why aren't those collars finished? How can the orders get out?" On and on, he rants at us, blaming the machinists for everything.

We are all going at full speed. Rosie comes down to our floor to pick up more pieces, winks at me, and hurries back upstairs. It must be 4:30 p.m. Here comes Anna Gullo to distribute our pay. *Good, only fifteen more minutes till quitting time!*

I tuck my envelope in my stocking top, the way Rosie does. I have just finished my last collar. My workbasket is empty for the first time this afternoon. I glance towards Malka. She is still busy, her head bent. Over at cutting table two, Isidore Abramowitz reaches for his coat. He keeps it hanging from a peg, under the shelf holding three fire buckets. There are more than two hundred of them, spread all around the factory floors.

Cutters keep their jackets close by so they can be the first ones out at the end of the day. Their assistants finish preparing the tables for Monday. The sheerest fabric, lawn, and tissue paper are stretched across the tabletops. The men stand and chat, waiting for the quitting bell. One of the cutters lights up a cigarette, right below the NO SMOKING sign.

There goes the bell. The power is shut off, and the machines are still. We are free at last. I get up gratefully. For a few seconds, the room is silent, then the hubbub begins. Chairs are pushed back, scraping noisily on the wooden floors. Talk is about the evening ahead of us.

Nettie, who still sits next to me, says, "I'm meeting my future mother-in-law for the first time. I'm so nervous."

"Don't be – she will like you, I'm sure," I say.

We make our way, one by one, down the aisle to the dressing room. Mr. Bernstein calls me over to the bookkeeper's desk, before I can get my coat. Dinah Lipschitz sits between two of the short cutting tables in front of the windows leading to the fire escape.

Mr. Bernstein says, "Please tell Beckie Singer that we expect her to return on Monday, Miriam."

A terrified cry penetrates every corner of the room. "Fire, Mr. Bernstein, fire! I smell something burning!" Eva Harris, sister of Mr. Isaac Harris, runs screaming across to the desk from the middle of the shop floor. She shouts the words everyone dreads to hear.

Suddenly I see smoke and flames rising up from under the second table. All around the floor, girls start echoing Eva's shouts of "Fire, fire!"

Mr. Bernstein immediately crosses to Mr. Abramowitz's table at the Greene Street windows. A fire must have started in the bins. It is weeks since Mr. Levy, the rag dealer, has collected the scraps. Now the bins are full to overflowing. Cutters come running with buckets of water to douse the flames, which are growing faster than the men seem able to quench them.

Only seconds have passed since the quitting bell rang. I'm still here and Malka is too, standing at her table. *What is the matter with her? Why isn't she running away from the fire?* She is too close to the blaze. Girls jostle and push their way from the aisles into the dressing room, anxious to save their new spring outfits.

I'm going to have to get to Malka. The crowd of girls is piling up at the door of the partition leading to the staircase. I won't join them without Malka. I run back towards her, shouting her name. She looks up, shocked, as if woken abruptly from a dream.

Is she going to stand frozen like that forever? The way she did when we were little girls and the Cossacks came to burn the shtetl? Papa cannot come and save us this time. We have to save ourselves! I don't know how, or where, to go. *Oh, please, Malka, hurry up.* Slowly she walks towards me.

"Run, Malka, run," I shout and meet her halfway down the aisle. I grasp her wrist. "We must stay together, whatever happens."

Mr. Bernstein jumps up on a table. "Someone get the fire hose from the Greene Street stairwell. We need more water!" he bellows.

Everyone around us is yelling and pushing to get out by the Greene Street stairs as fast as they can. Girls call out in Russian, Yiddish, English, and Italian for their friends, their sisters, their mothers to help them. They shove, elbow, and kick their way out. Workers run in every direction, from the aisles into and out of the dressing room, to the windows, to the passenger elevators on the Washington Place side. Smoke fills the room. It is everywhere.

For the year I have worked here, not once has anyone told us what to do in case of an emergency. We twist and turn, retching and choking, making our way through heat and smoke. Sparks dart in every direction. The blaze comes nearer. That small tongue of flame from the bins has fanned out, catching hold of one fabric after another. Paper patterns flare up on the wire and fall on tables, onto chairs and wicker baskets. In some, the delicate fabric pieces left to be finished for Monday feed the greedy flames. Fire bursts out, flying from one surface to another, showing no mercy.

I tighten my hand on Malka's wrist as a rush of heat and flame comes roaring in. Windows explode. A fiery wave of heat spares no one. More girls crowd at the Greene Street partition. *How are we all to get through that narrow door before the fire engulfs us all?* There are over a hundred and eighty of us working on the eighth floor today.

Mr. Bernstein cries out, "There's no water coming out of the hoses."

Still at her desk, Dinah Lipschitz screams "Fire" into the phone, over and over, to alert those on the other floors. She looks up at me and points to the back wall, where someone has opened the center windows to the fire escape. The steel shutters, usually fastened shut, are pinned back. I have never seen them opened before. I pull Malka towards the windows and the single fire escape that serves the whole building. It is attached to the outside wall and starts at the tenth floor. There are girls ahead of us. I need both hands free to climb over the table blocking the window. I tell Malka to stay close behind me.

Then I crawl out of the window onto the skinny ledge of the balcony. From here, it is one step down onto the first rung of the narrow ladder. There is scarcely room for me to stand. Cautiously, I manage to get up and put one foot onto the slatted, sloping ladder. A girl a few steps ahead of me shouts something. I feel the ladder tremble with our weight. The ladder is flimsy, and I wonder if it will hold to the outside wall.

"Don't come any farther yet," she calls out. "Some girls have reached the sixth floor, and they say to wait." I am poised to go down, but now, step back. I need to tell Malka to stay where she is, but she is not behind me. Girls waiting at the windows scream at me to hurry. I crawl back along the ledge and climb in through the window. I look down the line of girls waiting to escape and ask if anyone has seen her.

I reach the crowd of girls crammed together at the exit to the Greene Street stairs. Mr. Bernstein frantically forces them through the narrow door of the partition. I shout, trying to get his attention to ask if he has seen Malka Pinski. He shakes his head and continues to save as many workers as he can from the inferno.

Did Malka get out? If not, where can she be? There is no place to hide. We are surrounded by walls of smoke and fire. *Was Malka looking for the Greene Street windows, longing for one more glimpse of sky?* No one could get though those sheets of flame. I call her name once more. She does not answer.

19

REDUCED TO ASHES

I can't breathe. The smoke rising from the smoldering wooden floors and chairs, and the flying sparks that singe my hair and clothes, are difficult to bear. Mr. Bernstein's shouts grow faint. Among the whoosh of the greedy roaring flames, I hear faint cries for help. *Could some of them be Malka's?*

I am disoriented. I shut my eyes for a second, trying to remember how the shop floor looked before the fire. I cough and cough, desperate for breath. Flames bar my way to the Greene Street exit. After I stumble, I crawl in the direction of the Washington Place door, praying it is the right way. I lift my skirt to protect my face from burning rags and debris, groping inch by inch towards a last way out. If I am wrong, then I, too, am lost. I reach the door. A group of girls are there before me.

"Malka, are you here?" I shout. Again, there is no answer.

Girls nearest to the front beat, kick, and push at the Washington Place door. It will not open. We know the door is always kept locked in working hours. The key hangs beside the door, and only the bosses may unlock it.

"The key is in the lock," someone shouts. "Why won't it turn?" The top half of the door is made of glass, crisscrossed by wire. The girls pressed against it beg us not to push so hard. They shout and plead, afraid their faces will be cut by broken glass. *How can we stop, when the flames come ever closer?* Fire corners us like animals about to be slaughtered. We are in a frenzy to get out, to break down the door.

A voice from behind us bellows, "Let me through! I'll get you out. Stay still." It is Louis Brown, senior machinist. He forces his way through, throwing us aside to get to the door. He reaches it and turns the key.

"It is opening," the girls call out as he pulls the door inwards.

"Don't push," he shouts, "or you will close it again." We girls at the back surge forward, leaning against those in front. We cannot help ourselves. Waves of heat threaten our backs. The weight of our bodies, straining to get out, closes the door again. All the factory doors open inwards, for the stairways are too narrow for them to open outwards.

At last, with flames only inches away, Mr. Brown wrenches the door open and we tumble through. Our clothes are scorched, our hair singed. Some girls have burns on their face and hands. My arms are scraped, my fingers blistered, but we are out of the furnace. I think only moments were left before the flames would have consumed us.

We start our descent down poorly lit, winding, narrow stairs. There is room for only one of us at a time. *How long has it been since the quitting bell?* I can't tell if it is only minutes or hours. I cling to the hope that Malka will miraculously appear. She might be waiting down below. Perhaps, at the last moment, she got through the partition door. *Did the ninth-floor girls get out in time? Was a warning given? Rosie, please be safe. Please let the Four Fates find each other again!*

It is impossible to hurry. *If only the steps were wider!* Yet some girls grasp at a hand to hold for comfort, slowing the descent still more. Suddenly we can go no farther. Crying and gasping for air, we are held up at the seventh floor by a woman or girl slumped across the steps. I try to edge around her, others to step over her. The air is full of smoke. The fire will soon catch up with us. Feet thunder up from below. Voices reach us.

"It's Police Officer Meehan," someone calls. We all know him – I have seen him riding his horse around Washington Square Park. He props the girl up against the wall, so we can get by. She has fainted. I recognize her – it is Eva Harris, the boss's sister, who called out "Fire." She must have gotten out right away – unlocked the door and left the key in the lock.

At the sixth floor, there are cries, shouts, and pounding coming from behind the door of a garment factory closed on a Saturday. We do not stop, but as we continue down, we hear Officer Meehan kick through the door.

We reach the lobby of Washington Place at last. It is filled with crying girls, police, doctors, and firefighters. They hold us back, afraid that we will be injured by things falling outside from the upper floors. *What things, bales of cloth?* As more eighth-floor girls come down from the stairs, they tell us they'd climbed down the fire escape to the sixth floor. They managed to smash a window there and clamber through, but had not dared to go down any farther. They had seen that the fire-escape ladder ended not on the street, but above a basement skylight. The smoke-filled yard was surrounded by a spiked iron fence. Afraid to fall into that black pit, they were trapped behind the locked sixth-floor door until Officer Meehan released them.

Numbly we cross the street after a short wait. Ambulances drive up, and fire wagons pulled by horses that rear and whinny stop close to the building. Workers from nearby and ordinary people come in groups to stand and watch. The crowd grows bigger. I lean against a storefront and wait, slumping on the sidewalk. Everything hurts. I close my eyes and say a silent prayer for friends and fellow workers.

When I hear cries and gasps from the watching crowd, I open my eyes and wish I had kept them closed.

Voices scream, "Don't jump! Wait." Girls are leaping from the window ledges of the ninth floor, their hair and skirts ablaze, their arms entwined. They jump in twos and threes, holding hands, or one by one. I put my hands over my ears to shut out the sound of bodies landing on the pavement. They sound as though they are bundles of soiled laundry dropping on a kitchen floor. I dare not think of Rosie and Malka.

I can't look away. Firemen run and bring life nets, spreading them out tightly beneath the jumping factory workers. But the nets are not strong enough to catch the falling bodies. The dead sprawl in ever increasing heaps.

The street is littered with pocketbooks, with hats and keepsakes and coins. The dreadful thuds continue. My face is wet with tears.

Finally, arms embrace me. "Miriam, you are safe! Thank God." Rosie makes the sign of the cross. "Where is Malka?" she says, looking around, expecting to see us together.

"I don't know. We started out together, but we got separated. I called her name and asked everyone I saw if they'd seen her. I looked for her as long as I could, but the fire was too fierce. I don't know if she fell or jumped or if . . ."

I cry and cry. My chest hurts – from smoke, from heat, but mostly because my heart is breaking.

Rosie points towards the building. "Look, they have put the ladders up! Now they will save those still clinging to the window ledges."

The crowd groans – the ladders reach only to the sixth floor. A girl throws herself towards the top rung of a ladder thirty feet below her, but misses and falls on top of the growing heap of bodies. A doctor signals to ambulance workers for help to carry a woman away. *How can she still be alive?*

The streets fill with people desperate to find their loved ones, but police hold them back.

"Oh, Rosie, I could not have borne to lose you!" I say. We both see girls we know – Nettie, Annie, and Paula from the eighth floor. But many more from the ninth floor lie crumpled on the sidewalk, like broken dolls.

Rosie asks me how I got out. I tell her how Louis Brown got the Washington Place door open. I want to curse the doors that open in, which almost caused our death, and the skimpy balconies leading to the treacherous fire escape.

An angry murmur runs through the crowd. The words spread fast from one person to another. "The fire escape collapsed. I saw it twist and break with my own eyes. Escape route? More like a death trap, if you ask me," a man says.

"The bodies were thrown off," another says.

A woman grabs a policeman's arm. "My girl, where is she? I want my daughter, Bella. Give me my little girl." He beckons to a neighboring woman, who leads her away.

A hush falls. We watch, mesmerized, as a young man on the ninth-floor ledge holds out his arm, as if to invite a young lady to step into a carriage. She steps, not into a carriage but into space. He helps another and another, and then the last girl kisses him before she leaps and he follows. Another gasp, as a girl – her skirt and hair burning – leaps down, her clothes catching on a pole protruding two floors below the Triangle Waist Company sign. She hangs there, burning before our eyes, then falls to the ground below.

A man standing next to us says it is only half an hour since the fire brigades arrived. Water from the fire hoses hurls endlessly against the building. The streams of water pooling in the gutters are stained red with the blood of those who lie on the sidewalk. Some bodies still smolder.

Across the street, the dead are being covered with tarpaulins by doctors and police.

"So many dead," Rosie whispers in horror.

20

ZAYDE'S BOOTS

Smoke rises above the Asch Building, blackening the sky. I want to go home, but am too afraid of what I'll see when I close my eyes. *Will anyone who heard the thud of falling bodies ever forget? How could so many die in such a short time?*

It is not dark yet as we wait for news of Malka. More and more people arrive. They have come in the thousands. The clanging of fire engines and the sight of flames and smoke over the skyscraper have spread word of the disaster. Police gather up the scattered possessions dropped or thrown by falling girls: coins, purses, necklaces, hats, and small mementos. They place them carefully in baskets and take them away.

Mrs. Singer arrives. "Miriam, Rosie, thank God you're alive!" she says. Beckie is with her and throws herself into our arms. Then, taking off her shawl, Beckie places it around my shoulders. Mrs. Singer wraps hers around Rosie. "Come," Mrs. Singer says, "now I take you both home."

I see Mrs. Pinski turn the corner into Greene Street. She is followed by Papa and Reuven. My father searches the crowd for me. He calls my name, "Miriam!"

"Papa, I am here."

He runs to me and holds me as he and Zayde used to do when I was a little girl, to comfort me from my nightmares. I remember the day of the pogrom, when we lived in the shtetl still, and how he and Malka's papa carried us to safety. I wish Malka could be safe again. *Why I am standing here without her?* If this were a bad dream, by morning it would be over.

Mrs. Pinski cries out, "Where is Malka? She must be on her way home. Go, Reuven, see if you can catch up with your sister. I don't want her to be afraid."

I take Mrs. Pinski's hand. She looks at me, waiting for me to speak. I don't know how to tell her that Malka has not come out of the building. I whisper the words and try not to wince at the pain of my burns as she squeezes my hand. She sees the tears in my eyes.

"She will come soon, Miriam. Malka is often late," her mother says. Finally, when I do not reply, Mrs. Pinski looks at me. She understands. Turning away from us, she runs across the street. She attempts, as so many others have, to break through the police cordon.

"Malka, come to Mama. Where are you? Come, darling, no need to hide." Papa and Reuven bring her back.

"We should go to the Mercer Street Police Station and find out if there is any news of Malka there," Beckie says.

The station is only three blocks away. When we arrive, there are hundreds of people ahead of us. After a long wait, we reach the entrance, but a line of policemen, guarding the door, keeps us from going in. We are told that all the bodies have been taken to a temporary morgue on the Twenty-sixth Street pier. It will open at midnight, and we should come back then. The word "morgue" makes me tremble.

We walk home. Papa says he will call for Mrs. Pinski and go with her and Reuven. I think about what I will tell Mama about the fire when she comes.

It grew dark, Mama. The fire was out in the building, but still the firemen and police were there. Lights blazed. We saw shadows move on the blackened floors. Then the firemen lowered bodies, wrapped in tarpaulins, down the side of the building. Firemen stood at the gaps, which only hours ago were windows. They made sure the bodies did not bump against the walls. They were so gentle with our friends, Mama. All I could think of was, why were not more of us given a chance to escape?

When I see Mrs. Pinski and Reuven enter their home and close the door without Malka, it breaks my heart again. We walk in silence until we reach our own building.

Beckie cries out: "I should have been with you! I could have helped. I feel so ashamed I stayed home for a hurt finger. I will never forgive myself. I hope they punish those 'Shirtwaist Kings' as they deserve. They are murderers! We should have refused to work behind locked doors and demanded more than one useless fire escape. I will never work for Blanck and Harris again. Rosie, Miriam, I am so sorry I persuaded you to come to the 'Triangle.'"

Beckie weeps. Mrs. Singer takes her back into their apartment. Papa cleans and bandages my wounds and sends us to bed. Rosie cries a little, then settles down. I close my eyes, and even though I changed my clothes when I got home, the smell of burning stays in my nose and throat.

"Miriam, can you sleep?" Rosie says. "I can't."

"I'll make some tea for us. It won't take a minute to reheat the water." We go to the kitchen, and Rosie sits down at the table. I pour our tea.

"Rosie, I have not asked you how you got out of the fire. I am so selfish, not thinking about what you have been through."

She says, "The moment the quitting bell rang, I went into the dressing room. My hair was falling down. The other girls came in, and we were laughing and teasing each other. One of the girls showed us a new dance step, and we tried it out. Esther showed off her new engagement ring. With all the 'oohs' and 'aahs,' we didn't hear any warning of the fire.

"When we came out, someone shouted, 'Fire!' At the same time, we saw flames at the windows. They shattered the glass and poured in. We panicked. Flames swept over the clothes on the examination table into the aisles, on everything in sight. The Greene Street door was jammed with girls trying to get out. Flames were coming up the stairs. I was near the window leading to the fire escape. I had only seen it once, when the shutters were open. I am afraid of heights, and there were other girls in front of me, jostling for space. I didn't know what to do or where to go."

"Imagine if you had been on that fire-escape ladder, Rosie. Thank goodness you did not climb out there and fall, when it collapsed," I say.

"I saw girls running to the Greene Street windows and those facing Washington Place. They were trying to get to the window ledges, their hair and clothes burning. There was nowhere else to go; fire was everywhere. Somehow I managed to reach the only other way out. I remembered the Washington Place door. I called to the girls to go there. Some were able to get through the flames. We hurled ourselves against the door. You know how that door is always kept locked? The key hangs beside it, for the bosses to come and go. Today it was not there.

"Suddenly, like a miracle, the passenger elevator stopped on our floor. The door opened, and I fell inside. Crowds of other terrified, screaming girls clambered on and over me. There were so many of us, the elevator doors would not close. I was afraid of being pushed through the open door against the wall of the shaft. Cries of 'Wait!' and the sound of girls hitting the roof of the elevator followed us down.

"That was the last journey the elevators made. They broke down, buckling from the heat of the flames. Gaspar Mortillalo and Joseph Zito are heroes. They made many trips, saving hundreds of us.

"Miriam, we were the last ones. There was no other way out for those left behind."

Papa comes in to the kitchen. "Miriam and Rosie, you need to rest. I am going to meet Mrs. Pinski and Reuven. Try to sleep."

Rosie heads back to bed.

"Papa, I want to go with you," I say.

"The morgue is no place for you, Miriam. I cannot allow it. You have been through enough."

"Papa, please. I have to go – she was my friend. I need to find out for myself what happened to her."

"Then come, Miriam, we'll go together."

We step out into the street. Many of our neighbors are going to the same place as we are. So many families from the Lower East Side must have lost relatives. Reuven and Mrs. Pinski wait for us outside their tenement building.

Papa offers Mrs. Pinski his arm, and Reuven walks on her other side. He says he has checked Belleview and St. Vincent's hospitals. Malka was not there.

"Our only hope is to find her body to bury," Reuven says. I wonder how we will all endure what lies ahead.

We walk along Misery Lane towards the river and join the crowd waiting for the gates of the morgue to open. A few years ago, a ship caught fire in the harbor and the dead were brought here, to this ugly shed. If I believed in ghosts, this is where they'd walk. The only sounds are of water lapping the sides of the pier, a few seagulls crying like mourners, a sob or two in the hushed crowd.

The gates swing open, and a policeman calls to us to enter. At first, the crowd makes no move, apprehensive of what is inside, before shuffling into the dim hall. Policemen stand at intervals, holding lanterns aloft. No light comes in from the few windows set high on the walls. I look at everything, except the bodies, before I realize I must look. That is why I am here – to find my friend.

We walk very slowly between the rows of bodies. They lie covered by sheets, in wooden boxes. Their heads are visible, supported by boards. I hold Mrs. Pinski's hand; she is dry-eyed. Occasionally there is a cry, a moan, or someone faints.

We stop at a wooden coffin towards the end of a row. A policeman draws closer and holds up his lantern for us. It is Malka. We recognize her only by her boots.

I cannot look at Malka's charred face. Mrs. Pinski sinks to the floor beside her daughter. Papa has one arm around Reuven's shoulders. I clutch Papa's other hand. The policeman shuts the lid of the box and writes Malka's name on a yellow card.

At home, Rosie is waiting for us. "Was she there? How did you . . . ?" she asks.

"Malka was wearing Zayde's boots," I say and cry on her shoulder.

Days later, we find out that one hundred and forty-six people died that night and many more were injured. Most of the girls who perished were from the ninth floor. The warnings came far too late. The funerals are over now.

At night, I am afraid to go to sleep. "Papa, I don't know what to do." I tell him how hard it is to get through the days and nights.

"Go on, however hard it is. That is all we can do after a great sorrow. Be patient, in time it will get easier. You have been spared, and now you owe it to those who were not to live a full life."

I try. Today, I take down the single candlestick, knowing that soon the second one will stand beside it. In June, Mama will be here. I polish the candlestick until my arm aches and my fingers are black. My blisters are healing, and soon only small scars will remain.

Mama will be dazzled when she lights the candles. I
decide to make a welcome present – a dress for Devora –
and ask Rosie to help me.

"You are so good at bargaining, Rosie. Come with me."
We go to Hester Street and decide on a length of sky blue
cotton. Rosie wheedles a matching blue ribbon from the
salesman. For the first time in days, we talk and laugh. It is
almost like old times.

As I cut and stitch the fabric, I think about my lost friend
. . . how we played together when we were small . . . how
happy we were to find each other again.

A month has passed by – it is almost the end of April.
Mama will be here soon. I cross off the days on the cal-
endar. Rosie starts work in a bakery on Hester Street next
week. Now that my hands are better, I have enrolled in a
class for shorthand and typing. Beckie is joining me. Papa
tells me not to worry about the money. He has finally been
promoted, and, as a cutter, his wages are much better.

Tonight it is Rosie's turn to make supper. I set the table.
Papa has returned home from work. He changes into the
shirt I had washed and pressed for him earlier. There is a
knock on the door. This is a strange time for a visitor. It won't
be Marco. He told Rosie that he is working nights this week.

I open the door. I just stand there, unable to speak. Then
I scream for Papa.

"Mama, oh, Mama, you are here at last!" There is pandemonium – laughing, crying, kissing, and hugging – as she and Devora come inside.

"Sam, without your beard, you look so young," Mama says. "Different, but handsome too."

"My Sara, you are just as I remember you."

A small hand tugs at my skirt. I look down at my sister. How beautiful she is with her dark eyes and curly hair.

"Who are you?" I say, pretending not to know her.

"I am Devora, and I am three." She holds up three fingers.

"I cannot believe it. My sister is only little, not a big girl like you."

"It is me. Look." She shows me the doll I gave her before I left.

I pick her up and twirl her around. "I have a present for you, Devora. After supper, I will give it to you. Look, here is your papa."

She runs to him, not a bit shy. He carries her to his chair and holds the tiny girl on his knee.

"Tomorrow, Papa will take you to play in the park. I will buy you an ice cream! Would you like that?" he asks.

"Don't start by spoiling her, Sam," Mama says, but she is smiling.

"A little spoiling doesn't hurt, Sara. I must make up for the three years I have missed."

There is another rap on the door. *Is it Yuri, who has been hiding to surprise us?*

"May I come in?" a deep voice says as I pull open the door. It is Kolya, arriving with the rest of Mama's luggage. He sets it down.

"You have grown up, Miriam. I have thought of you so often." I blush, tongue-tied.

Rosie comes in, carrying a huge plate of spaghetti. Now she sets a place for Kolya. She and Mama are already talking together like old friends.

We eat and share our news. Mama says, "Yuri will come when he finishes school. He will be fourteen then, and this time he will answer the emigration officer's questions, I am sure. Bubbe and Zayde send so much love. Who knows, they might change their minds and come with their beloved Yuri."

Kolya leaves after supper. He is boarding with an old friend, who lives nearby on East Fourth Street. Mama invites him for Sabbath night dinner.

On Friday night, when Mama lights the candles, the flames cast a special glow on the faces around the table. The candlesticks gleam on the best white tablecloth, which Mama brought with her. I did not think I could ever be happy again, but I am.

I will never forget you, Malka. I will remember you, not consumed by fire, but reaching for the sky.

Berlin, Germany, 1933

Epilogue

BURN!

Herr Ludwig has set our class a composition. The title is *My Family and I*. We have to hand it in tomorrow. I'll begin by writing my name and age.

I am Peter Schmidt, and I will be ten years old next month, on May 3, 1933. Herr Ludwig told us to write truthfully. If I do that, I'd write that my stepfather looks at me as if I am an unwanted dog. He makes me feel like a stray that has wandered in from the gutter. When he's at home, I do my best to become invisible. I'd better not say that!

I can write that my stepfather is an officer in the SS and describe how tall he looks in his black uniform. I can write that Maria, our maid, has to polish his boots every night. She spits on them to make them shine. If I said that I think she does not really like cleaning them, it might get us both in trouble.

My stepfather is considered to be very handsome. He has blond hair and blue eyes. My four-year-old half sister, Helga, looks just like him. She's a nice kid, and it's not her fault that she's his pet. He tells everyone she is Hitler's ideal, a pure-blooded German child. When he lashes out at whatever doesn't please him – often me – my mother lowers her eyes and says nothing. I hate him. I can't write that. I'd be kept in for a week or get caned for being disrespectful!

Today is April 1, 1933, the day the nation has been told not to buy from Jews. My stepfather reminded us of the boycott at breakfast, but I forgot all about it. I had a five-pfennig coin burning a hole in my pocket and planned to buy a chocolate bar after school. I remembered the boycott when, on the way home, every Jewish shop I passed was plastered with yellow stars and slogans: GERMANS, DO NOT BUY FROM JEWS. THE JEW IS YOUR ENEMY.

I often buy chocolate from Herr Friedlander. He is nice and sometimes gives me a treat for Helga. When I ignored the warnings and opened his shop door as usual, suddenly someone grabbed my collar. He spun me round and threw me down on the cobblestones. "Not learned to read yet? Get home before I give you something to remember."

The Brownshirt kicked me, smirking at a few passersby, who looked the other way. I picked myself up, grabbed my satchel, and ran home. Maria screamed when she saw the blood trickling down my knees. As she cleaned me up, I had to listen to a lecture about not fighting, but she gave me a big piece of cake with my glass of milk. Maria has been our maid forever. She is very kind to Helga and me, especially me.

Boycott Jewish business day? I've never heard anything so ridiculous. Mother has our shoes mended at Herr Israel's shop, Boot and Shoe Repair. With a name like Israel, of course he's a Jew. *Who cares?* I am one, too.

It's almost dinnertime. I'd better get started on my homework. Some of what I write will be the truth.

My Family and I

My real name is not Peter Schmidt. It is Peter Markov, the name of my father, Yuri Markov. He was born in Russia and came to Berlin when he was a boy. He became a soldier in the 1914–18 war and enlisted when he was seventeen. He served in Belgium and France and received a medal for bravery under fire.

My father was wounded in the Battle of Ypres. That's how he met my mother. She nursed him at the Belgian hospital where he was sent to recover from his wounds. They were married after the war, and I was born in 1923. When I was a year old, my father died. I will be ten years old this year.

My mother married Georg Werner Schmidt, my step-
father, in 1927, when I was four years old. He is a high-
ranking officer in the SS and was personally promoted
by Chancellor Adolf Hitler.

I have two photographs of my real father, the first one
taken in 1916. He is in a soldier's uniform. We look alike
– we are both skinny with black hair. The second one is of
my father with his grandparents. He is holding me on his
knee, and I am just a baby. His grandparents died of the
Spanish Flu, five years before my father.

My most precious possession is my father's medal, which
I keep in my desk with my stamp collection. I have relatives
in New York, America, whom I have never met. Every year,
they send me a birthday card. I keep the cards and save the
stamps for my collection.

My stepfather has forbidden me to reply to my American
relatives. He refers to them as "those Jews."

Maria sounds the gong for dinner. I'll finish my homework later. I have only a bit more to write, about my favorite
sports, which are skating and swimming. I am saving up
for a bicycle. I remember to wash my hands before I go
downstairs, as my stepfather always inspects my hands.

Tonight, we're having boiled tongue, cabbage, and mashed
potatoes – my stepfather's favorite. The smell is as bad as
the taste of the pink meat, which makes me feel sick.

His "jokes" are worse than the meal. "I wonder whose mouth this tongue came from," he says. Or, "Why so quiet? Has the cat got your tongue?" I can't bring myself to laugh, like Mother and Helga. The jokes weren't even funny the first time I heard them. Now he repeats them every time the boiled tongue appears. His laugh is the loudest.

Tonight, he cuts me the fattest slice. On purpose, I bet. I eat some potato and a bit of the cabbage. When he has stopped paying attention to me and has turned to Mother, I hide the tongue under the cabbage. Maria removes the dinner plates, including mine, and brings in dessert. It's apple strudel and vanilla sauce. I think I've got away with it this time, but no such luck!

"Do you think I'm blind and stupid, boy? Maria, Peter will not be having dessert, today or any other day, until he has finished his food. You will serve it to him at every meal until he has done so. Is that understood?"

"Yes, sir," Maria curtsies and goes out.

Helga starts to cry. Mother takes her on her knee. "Papa is not cross with you, darling," she says. "Peter is the naughty one, wasting good food."

"Now see what you've done – upset your mother and your sister and ruined the meal. You are a first-class trouble-maker, like the rest of your kind. Don't you understand how lucky you are, a little Jew, allowed to live in my house? The situation is becoming intolerable. Elsa, my coffee, please.

I have a meeting tonight, concerning the Jewish problem. Damn it, boy, leave the room."

Mother bites her lip. Her hands shake as she pours my stepfather's coffee. I get up and, without looking at him, slide my chair under the table, fold my napkin, and go upstairs.

I wait until I hear Mother say good-bye to my stepfather in the hall and the front door shut. My bedroom window overlooks the street. Almost every building displays the Nazis' red and white flag, with its black swastika. A sleek black car draws up in front of our house. The SS chauffeur gets out. My stepfather walks down the steps, and they exchange the Hitler salute. The car speeds off.

What a relief! Now I can close my bedroom door. The only time I have any privacy is when he's out of the house. My stepfather has forbidden me to shut my door.

"If your son has nothing to hide, why does he need to close the door?" he once said. Mother did not reply, as usual. However, she ignores my closed door when he is out. I decide to write to my relatives tonight. I can buy a stamp on my way to school.

Dear Aunt Miriam,

I want to thank you for all the birthday cards. I treasure them. Please don't send me anymore, because they get me in trouble with my stepfather. I have a photograph of my real father, Yuri. I think we look alike. When I am

grown up, as soon as I leave school, I will earn money
and come and visit you.
  Best wishes to everyone from
  Peter Markov

On my birthday, I watch for the postman. No card arrives
from America, so my letter got there in time. Now I can
enjoy my birthday dinner of roast chicken and chocolate
cake. Mother gives me five marks towards my bicycle fund,
and Helga gives me a tin of peppermints. I ask Maria to wrap
a piece of cake for my friend Simon Frankel. He told me his
father, who is a professor of mathematics, was fired from his
position at the University of Berlin because he is a Jew.

Since then, Simon has not joined in the Hitler salute.
Now that Adolf Hitler is chancellor of Germany, all students
must greet their teachers with "*Heil Hitler*" and salute the
leader's portrait. Simon finds all kinds of ways to get out
of joining in. He comes in a few minutes late with some
excuse, or pretends to have a coughing fit or a sudden need
to blow his nose, or bends down to tie his shoelaces.

Simon sits at the end of the back row, and as I sit in the
middle, I can see him out of the corner of my eye. Today he
doesn't even pretend but stands up straight, mouth closed,
arms by his side.

Herr Ludwig explodes: "Frankel, I have had enough of
your willful disobedience. Come here." Some of the boys

snicker. The teacher raises his cane and brings it down hard, five times on each hand. Simon winces but doesn't cry. I wish I was as brave as him. By recess, his fingers are red and swollen. I follow him into the washroom and run the cold tap.

"I'm sorry," I say.

"Why? You're all right, nice and safe with a father in the SS."

I want to punch him. Instead, I warn him, "Don't ever say that again. He's not my father, he's my stepfather, and you know it. My father and my grandparents were Jewish too."

Simon blows on his hands to dry them. "If you swear not to say anything to anyone, Peter, I'll tell you a secret."

"I swear. I can keep a secret."

"This is my last day at this rotten school. My father has been offered a job at the Sorbonne, in Paris. We're leaving tomorrow. He'll be teaching again, safe from the Nazis. They can't do anything to us in France."

"I'm glad, Simon. Best of luck – I'll miss you." We shake hands. He winces. I'm an idiot, forgetting about his hands for a minute.

On my way home from school, as I'm nearing Opera Square, opposite the university, I smell fire. There is shouting and laughter. A crowd of Hitler Youth are joking around with some Brownshirts. They hurl books onto a huge bonfire.

People come from every direction, with armfuls of volumes to throw into the flames.

"Hey, kid, give us a hand," a tall boy in uniform says, thrusting a stack of books into my arms. I mutter something about being late for my piano lesson, drop the books, and walk away as fast as I can. They've all gone crazy – no one burns books.

A voice yells, "When we've finished burning books, we'll start on the Jews." They start to chant, "Burn the Jews! Burn the Jews!" I run all the way home, afraid they'll come after me. I've been beaten up a couple of times in the playground because I'm friends with Simon. I wish I had a bike. I wish I could go to America.

That evening at supper, my stepfather is in an unusually good mood. He leans back in his chair, smiling at Mother.

"Elsa, children, remember this day, May 10, 1933. All over Germany, throughout the night, patriotic Germans will join together to burn books that print lies. It is a great day for our country. We will not rest until every page that besmirches our great leader's work is reduced to ashes."

I feel cold, and my teeth chatter. Mother puts her hand on my forehead and asks Maria to make me a hot drink. "You must have caught a chill, Peter," she says.

"You baby him, Elsa," my stepfather says. "We'll take Helga out to watch the book burning without him. It is a sight not to be missed."

"If you don't mind, dear, I will leave Helga at home. The crowds might frighten her. Go up to bed, Peter."

Back in my room, I get into bed and huddle under the blankets. I can't help wondering, *Will I end up like the books?* Simon is lucky to be going to France.

One afternoon, Mother has been listening to me practice the piano when she is called to the telephone. She comes back smiling.

"That phone call was from an acquaintance. She is on holiday in Berlin and has asked us to have tea with her, on Saturday, at the Hotel Adlon. As Georg will be at a rally in Munich this weekend, Maria can take Helga to the zoo. What a nice outing for the two of us, Peter." I think it's a treat to have a whole weekend without my stepfather. I can't remember the last time Mother and I went out together.

On Saturday, Mother makes me wear my best suit. The Hotel Adlon is one of the smartest hotels in the city. It is right by the Brandenburg Gate and overlooks Unter den Linden, where all the parades take place. Mother gives our names to the man at the desk. We are expected, and he sends a bellboy to take us up in the elevator. The door of the suite opens at the first knock. I look up at a tall gentleman and a beautiful dark-haired lady.

"Frau Schmidt and Peter, how very nice to meet you. I am Kolya Seltzovsky, and this is my wife, Miriam – your aunt Miriam, Peter." We all shake hands. *I can't believe it – my relatives from America? Why are they here, and why didn't Mother tell me?* I hope they don't mention my letter to them.

"I have been looking forward so much to meeting you both, Frau Schmidt," my aunt says.

"Please, call me Elsa," Mother replies.

In no time at all, we are seated at a round table. Beside it is a huge cake stand, laden with little sandwiches, chocolate éclairs, and fruit tarts. There is a big apple strudel and a dish of whipped cream. A waiter pours coffee and tea and brings me a glass of lemonade, before leaving us alone. I feel too shy to speak, but not too shy to eat!

After tea, Aunt Miriam and Mother exchange family photographs. They admire each other's children. I look at a photo of the cousins I have never met, Jacob and Rachel, who are ten and eight, Aunt Miriam tells me. There are many other people in the photographs.

Aunt Miriam points to them one by one. "These are your grandparents, Peter – Samuel and Sara. Here are my dear friends Beckie and Rosie, with their husbands, Reuven and Marco, and their children. We met when we first came to America. Together, we started a clothing store for girls, called Malka's Dresses."

She hands Mother a card. "If you give me Helga's measurements, Elsa, I'd be delighted to send her one of our dresses. Look, Peter, this is your aunt Devora. She was born when your father was the same age as you. My sister designs and makes dolls. Each dress comes with a small doll, tucked into the pocket."

"Helga's favorite color is blue," I tell my aunt.

"Peter resembles Yuri so much as a boy," Uncle Kolya says.

Aunt Miriam puts her hand over my mother's. "I know how much he loved you, Elsa," she says. The handkerchiefs come out, and that is when the real conversation begins. *Why are they crying, after such a lovely tea?* Uncle Kolya says that I may choose some pastries to take back for Helga and me!

"Miriam," Mother says, "after Yuri died, times were very difficult. I was left alone with a baby. There was no work, often not enough food to eat. . . ." Mother dabs her eyes. I have never heard her speak of this before.

"In 1927, Germany was not like it is now. When I married Georg, it seemed the right thing to do. Peter needed a father and a real home," Mother says.

"Yes, I can see that much has changed. You must wonder why Kolya and I have come to Germany, and why we wanted to meet you," Aunt Miriam says. Mother nods.

Aunt Miriam continues, "We are here to bring Kolya's brother, Lev, back with us. We sail from Southampton, England, on the White Star Liner RMS *Georgic*, in three days."

Uncle Kolya says, "I own a printing and small publishing press. My brother is an expert bookbinder and printer of Hebrew texts. He will be a great help in my work. We have a spare ticket for Peter, if he would like to return to New York with us. That is, if you permit it and if he wants to go."

Aunt Miriam says, "Elsa, I can only imagine how difficult it is for you to raise a half-Jewish child in Germany, at this time. There would be no problem with obtaining a visa for him. Peter is the son of a war hero and the nephew of American citizens. We would be taking him for a visit, to meet his family. Elsa, if you agree to this . . . holiday, Peter's stay can be extended permanently. He would be educated with his cousins and given every advantage. We have a home in Brooklyn, New York, and a summer cottage in Maine. The children camp, swim, and ride. We all want Peter to come with us. We would do our very best to make Yuri's son happy. We can keep him safe, Elsa."

I'm not sure I understand. *Are they saying I can go to America?* I look at Mother.

She says, "You have taken me by surprise. I don't know what to say, Miriam, I am overwhelmed. I had no idea. . . ."

"Do you mean leave, leave Germany forever?" I ask Aunt Miriam.

"I don't know the answer to that, Peter. I think it would be for a long time, until things are different here. Now, Uncle Kolya and I are going to go out on the balcony to look at the beautiful view of the city. You and your mother can speak in private and discuss our suggestion." They leave us alone.

"Peter, I am sorry. You are very young to have to make such a hard decision. Yuri always regretted that he did not go to America. I loved him very much, and I love you, and whatever you decide, I will understand." *Is Mother letting me choose?* I take a deep breath. I hope she won't be upset. I don't need to think about my answer at all.

"I want to go very much, Mother. I'll miss you and Helga and Maria, of course. I'll write to you often. Perhaps one day, you will come to America for a visit."

Two days later, I am packed and sitting in the car between my uncle and aunt. It is the start of our long journey. My stepfather was delayed in Munich. Mother made me say good-bye to him on the telephone. We are both glad not to have to see each other again. I wave to Mother and Maria and Helga, until they are out of sight.

"Uncle Kolya," I say quietly, so that the chauffeur does not hear me. "I saw the Nazis burn books. I stood right by the fire and watched them."

"I know. No need to be afraid anymore, Peter. In America, we print books. We do not burn them."

Aunt Miriam says, "When Yuri and I were children, your grandfather used to say, 'In America, they don't let you burn.'" She and Uncle Kolya look at each other and smile.

I lean back against the car's leather upholstery and dream of all the things I will be allowed to do in America – play with my cousins, go to school and not have to sit in the back row, just because my father was Jewish. I can choose who and what I want to be.

Mother said my father wanted to go to America. I think he would be happy that I am making the journey. *I'm going for both of us, Papa.*

The End.

AFTERWORD

Family Markov, their friends and neighbors, and the people they encounter during their lifetime are imaginary. Their experiences in their quest for a better life are similar to those of many immigrants. Their story is played out against a backdrop of real events, side by side with the public figures of the time.

The following characters in the novel are based on themselves: Max Blanck and his wife, Bertha, Isaac Harris, Anna Gullo, Dinah Lipschitz, Isidore Abramowitz, Eva Harris, Samuel Bernstein, Louis Brown, Joseph Zito, Gaspar Mortillalo, Officer Meehan, Joseph Wexler, and Lena Goldman.

After the tragedy of the Triangle Waist Company fire of March 25, 1911, public outrage led to the creation of the Fire Investigating Commission. Two years of deliberation resulted in twenty-five new rules, which were passed into law in the state of New York. These included the following.

- The installation of automatic sprinklers
- Mandatory fire drills
- The regulation that doors are to open outwards and to remain unlocked during working hours
- The regular inspection of fire escapes for both maintenance and safety
- The regulation that fire escapes are not to end before reaching ground level and are to allow easy access, without furniture or sewing machines, obstructing exit doors

Max Blanck and Isaac Harris were brought to trial on December 4, 1911. Three weeks later, an all male jury acquitted them of manslaughter, in a verdict of NOT GUILTY. Blanck and Harris waited years before they agreed to pay seventy-five dollars for each of the 146 lives lost in the fire. However, the men's reputations were ruined. The days of the Shirtwaist Kings came to an end in 1914, when their partnership ended.

Adolf Hitler and the Nazi Party came to power in Germany in January 1933. The one-day boycott of Jewish businesses, and the burning of twelve thousand books deemed "anti-German," began a regime of terror that ended with the death of six million Jews.

April 5, 1933, saw the arrest of many of the inhabitants of the Scheunenviertel, the Barn Quarter. On November 9 and 10, 1938, during the pogrom of *Kristallnacht* – the Night of Broken Glass – over ten thousand Jewish inhabitants of the quarter were arrested and deported. Homes, places of worship, and shops were burned and looted. The life of a once-vibrant community was erased. Street names were changed, and no trace remains of what was once there.

ACKNOWLEDGMENTS

Thanks to the wisdom, encouragement, and patience of
Sue Tate, my editor, and to the entire Tundra team for
their ongoing support. Love and thanks to my family for
always being there for me.

Also, my grateful thanks to
Dr. Michael Berman
Deborah Hodge
Sarah and Reuven Levine
Ellen Schwartz
Nicholas Selo
Dr. John P. Wade
A.J. Watts